W9-BUN-850

the
wrap-up
list

STEVEN ARNTSON

HOUGHTON MIFFLIN HARCOURT
Boston   New York

Copyright © 2012 by Steven Arntson

All rights reserved. Originally published in hardcover in the United States by Houghton Mifflin Books for Children, an imprint of Houghton Mifflin Harcourt Publishing Company, 2012.

For information about permission to reproduce selections from this book, write to Permissions, Houghton Mifflin Harcourt Publishing Company, 215 Park Avenue South, New York, New York 10003.

www.hmhco.com

The text of this book is set in Fournier MT Std.

The Library of Congress has cataloged the hardcover edition as follows:
Arntson, Steven, 1973–
The wrap-up list / by Steven Arntson.
p. cm.
Summary: "When sixteen-year-old Gabriela's death is foretold by a letter, she must complete her 'wrap-up list' before she's forced to say goodbye." —Provided by publisher.
[1. Death—Fiction. 2. Hispanic Americans—Fiction.] I. Title.
PZ7.A7415Wr 2013
2012014035

ISBN: 978-0-547-82410-9 hardcover
ISBN: 978-0-544-23264-8 paperback

Manufactured in United States of America
DOC 10 9 8 7 6 5 4 3 2 1
4500464016

seven days before
departure day

death letter

Some people die from heart attacks, and some from falling off ladders. Some are killed in car accidents. Some drown. Some, like my grandfather Gonzalo, die in war.

But some people don't die — they depart. Whether this is a good or a bad thing is debatable, but departures are always interesting, so when the bell rings at the end of seventh period I'm not surprised that Iris springs up and places one pale hand firmly on my forearm. She digs her red nails in. "Hurry, Gabriela!" she says.

I allow myself to be pulled from the classroom as Mr. Harpting, our history instructor, hopelessly calls out a reading assignment to his former audience. Iris and I are already in the hall, and Harpting's voice is lost amid the afterschool rush.

Outside, cars and buses clog the sunny hilltop turnaround. Iris drags me down the front steps, her long, straight blond hair glowing like a beacon. At the entrance to the student parking lot, a voice behind us calls, "Where are you guys going?" I turn to see Sarena running to catch up, her trumpet case bouncing against one thigh. I explain as she reaches us: "Iris thinks the Singing Man's departing today—" I hold out my free hand to her, and she grabs on. Her braided black hair, lustrous in the afternoon sun, shines. She sings: *"Ca-a-a-ro mio be-e-e-n!"* reprising the song we heard the Singing Man perform yesterday. "Hey, Gabriela," she says, reminded, "did you think about those lyrics?"

I wince. "I'm sorry," I say. "I will."

"That's okay," she replies. She's disappointed, and I feel bad. Sarena plays trumpet and sometimes sings in her dad's band—a jazz orchestra called the Washington Fifteen, which is the house act at the Caballero Hotel downtown. Her dad told her she could compose a song for the group, and she asked me to write the lyrics, because she thinks I have a way with words. I was thrilled at first, but now I regret it. I can't seem to get started.

Iris pulls us both through the parking lot, where mostly juniors and seniors loiter, playing car radios and socializing. I see Sylvester Hale leaned against the hood of his new pepper red sports car—he's in his letterman's jacket, surrounded by friends who also wear letterman's jackets. His pretty, wide-set eyes glance my direction for a moment, and my legs wobble, but Iris keeps pulling, and soon we're past.

"Hey—" another voice calls.

"Grab him!" I say to Sarena. It's Raahi standing outside his beat-up hatchback with some friends. Raahi's older than the three of us, eighteen, a thin kid with a head of thick, wavy black hair. He's one of those rare seniors who don't mind being friends with underclassmen. I met him last year in Mr. Wilkson's American Geography class.

Sarena extends her hand, holding out her trumpet case. Raahi takes her wrist, turning us into a chain of four as we head down the hill, leaving Raahi's car. He doesn't even bother to lock it up.

The four of us are a known group at school. Once, when we were sitting in a row in art class (left to right: Iris, me, Raahi, and Sarena), Mr. Jensen spontaneously used our skin tones as an example of a color gradient. I feel strange about that, but I guess it's true — cream color, light brown, brown, dark brown. Our school isn't very diverse in this regard, so I guess it struck Jensen as a noteworthy moment of life mimicking art.

"Iris thinks the Singing Man is departing today," Sarena explains to Raahi.

He nods, mock serious, and says, "Iris thinks someone's departing *every* day."

"I heard that!" Iris yells over at us.

"One time she thought Ms. Lime was going to depart," I recall.

"Remember when she thought *I* was going to?" says Sarena.

"And last week it was Sylvester," I say, "because of his new car."

"But *how* did he get that car?" says Iris, trying laughingly to defend herself. "It appeared out of nowhere."

We arrive at the bottom of the hill, where Cougar Way intersects Eighth. I hear the Singing Man before I see him — a big, operatic voice that suggests the exact sort of person who comes into view across the street: an elderly, portly Italian gentleman. He's wearing a blue suit and a thin red tie. The first time we saw him, a few weeks ago, Iris was immediately sure he was going through his wrap-up, and when he kept performing each day, the rest of us were inclined to agree — the Singing Man was scheduled to depart.

Here's how departures work. First, you're contacted by one of the Deaths, the creatures who oversee the process, usually with a letter saying "Dear So-and-So, your days are numbered." Then you correspond, deciding how much time you need and what you want to wrap up before you're taken. In the Singing Man's case, he wanted to sing, obviously.

No one knows why Deaths select particular people. There are plenty of theories, but it's basically random beyond the fact of one statistic: departures account for one percent of all fatalities.

Sarena says all of the Singing Man's songs are famous Italian arias, with lyrics along the lines of "Don't leave — it's bad when you go." Today, he belts his a cappella melodies with particular gusto. "Have we heard this one?" I ask Sarena. The Singing Man's repertoire is pretty limited, but this melody is unfamiliar.

"No, we haven't," says Sarena.

"This is the day. *For sure!*" says Iris as a delivery truck rumbles past, interrupting our view. "He saved this song for today. It's his swan song."

As the truck exits the intersection and the Singing Man returns to view, my eyes widen.

No matter how many times you encounter them, the Deaths are startling creatures. The one who appears today is Gretchen, whom I've seen a few times before. Like all the Deaths, she's about eight feet tall, extremely skinny, and grayish silver, as if you're seeing her through a screen that filters the colors out. The Deaths live in a place called the Silver Side (where everything is presumably colored silver?) and only come visiting here when they're drawn for a departure. Today, Gretchen is wearing a dark gray jacket over a silvery, flowing, ankle-length dress, and slate-colored heels. She approaches slowly, walking like they all do, as if through water — for some reason the Deaths experience our atmosphere as if it's thick, and a little buoyant. They always look like they're crossing the bottom of a swimming pool. Gretchen's salt and pepper hair floats hugely around her, and her dress pushes and pulls against her frame, moved by unseen currents. She looks about fifty years old, but the Deaths are much older than they look (centuries, millennia in some cases). Her face, long and skinny, is expressionless, and my eyes are drawn to the dark slits, like gills, to either side of her nose.

"We're going to see it!" Iris whispers frantically. She clutches one of my hands in excitement.

Gretchen stands to one side while the Singing Man finishes his last song. A number of people see what's going on and stop to watch. When the Singing Man falls silent, no one applauds, but he bows. Then he turns to Gretchen. She extends one hand toward him, as if they're being introduced. He reaches out hesitantly, and their fingers close. The Singing Man straightens up — the way you might if an ice cube were dropped down the back of your shirt. He takes a deep, surprised breath.

Then, beginning at his hand where he's touching Gretchen and spreading through his body, everything about him from his pink skin to his blue coat to his red tie turns silvery gray. His eyes close, and he exhales. His thinning hair lifts slightly around him, weightless, submerged. He stands still for a few moments, and then his lids flutter, confused, until his gaze settles on Gretchen.

"Thank you," he says politely, his voice barely audible to me across the street. Then he and Gretchen turn together, and begin to walk away — toward the Fields.

"Let's go!" says Iris, excited.

I roll my eyes. *"Why* do you always have to follow them? I can't. I've got homework."

"Sarena?" says Iris, but Sarena holds up her trumpet case,

indicating her need to practice. "Raahi?" Iris sees his answer in his eyes, and without even a goodbye she rushes off, leaving us staring after her for the few moments it takes her to disappear up the street after her quarry.

"Want a lift home?" Raahi asks me. He gestures back up the hill to the parking lot, where his car is presumably still sitting with all the doors unlocked.

"No thanks, it's nice out," I say.

"Raahi," says Sarena, "have you gotten any more news?" Sarena always asks about this. I feel awkward broaching the subject, but for some reason she and Raahi seem able to talk about it.

"No," he replies. "I doubt there'll be any at this point."

"Have you started . . . packing?" I ask.

"A little," he says. "I'm not supposed to bring much. You get on the bus with just a duffel bag. But I'm putting away other stuff, for Mom — so she doesn't have to do it."

There's a lot in these words. Raahi doesn't say, for instance, *in case I don't come back,* though he's surely thinking it. He's said as much during the past few weeks.

Raahi has been drafted. He got his card last month, and he'll be leaving for basic training next Tuesday. In all honesty, I'm a little excited for him — jealous, even. I don't say it, because he's obviously scared, but it kind of sounds like an adventure. It has crossed my mind to volunteer when I'm old enough (I'm barely sixteen right now).

"Heading back up the hill?" Raahi asks Sarena.

"Yeah," she says.

"Can I carry your trumpet?"

"Sure, okay," says Sarena, handing it over.

The two of them say goodbye to me and head back up. I watch them go—short Sarena and lanky Raahi. Since he got his card, his demeanor has totally changed from what I've always known. I don't think I'd ever seen him in a bad mood before the last few weeks. He isn't the first senior at school to have his name come up, but he's the first who's a friend of mine.

I continue ruminating on the matter as I walk toward home. The U.S. isn't technically at war yet. A month and a half ago we closed our borders to people from countries with "questionable sympathies," but few shots have been fired. It's about looking tough for now. The most popular quote from the television pundits so far has been "Speak softly and carry a big stick," which President Roosevelt said over a century ago. Several commentators have pointed out the possibility that this African proverb originated in the very country we're about to attack. It's strange to think that the stick mentioned in that proverb is partly composed of seniors from Central High.

The other term that's discussed frequently is *victory*. When you go to war, it's important to have a clear sense of what you mean by *victory*, so you know when to stop fighting. Something about that strikes me funny. I imagine a football team arguing over the nature of victory. It seems kind of obvious. For instance, World War II: the free world fought against fascism. That's pretty clear. At school I learned that World War II is called the Good War.

World War II is the war my grandfather Gonzalo fought in. He disappeared somewhere in Africa, maybe Tunisia. He died serving his country, according to his conscience. I think he's a hero, and so do my dad and my aunt Ana. If I had the chance to make the same choice as Gonzalo, I'd follow his footsteps. I would fight.

Aunt Ana and Dad love to talk about Gonzalo. He was the son of a peasant farmer in Mexico, and spoke imperfect English. It's because of him that my grandmother Fidelia, whom I called Abuela, moved here; because of him that my dad was born here; because of him that I'm growing up here, barely sixteen years old and poised at the start of the next war.

I'm still thinking about Raahi when I reach my block. As I turn onto my street, I encounter a sudden and strong smell of flowers—hyacinths or hydrangeas (which is the one that blooms in early spring?). I breathe deep. It's one of my most favorite scents—not a nice, neat smell, but a kind of wild one. You have to wrestle with it. Sometimes it makes me sneeze, and it always sends my mind in romantic directions. I recall something Raahi told me the other day: that he has not been kissed. He's eighteen, about to ship off to war. For a moment, I imagine a fantasy for him in which a beautiful girl kisses him just as he's about to step onto a boat/plane/train.

Iris, who's my best friend, hasn't been kissed either. This is especially perplexing to me, because not only is she nice, funny, and unquestionably a knockout, but she was asked to freshman prom by nine different guys. She said no to all of them. I can't fault her for being picky — she deserves someone special — but even I went to freshman prom. Iris stayed home and played Scrabble with her parents.

My date to freshman prom was Norbert Ganz. We didn't kiss — we were just friends. I smile now thinking of Norbert, who doesn't even attend Central High anymore. I may not ever see him again, but I have the feeling that as I get older it will become pretty funny that the name of my date to freshman prom was Norbert Ganz. Norb, we called him.

My apartment building is an old five-story brick rectangle nestled between two other five-story brick rectangles. (They are all very nice rectangles, well-maintained and with pretty flourishes at each cornice.) I enter the lobby and walk the red carpet to the numbered mailboxes on the wall, by the long mirror. I watch my reflection pass across and observe myself. I'm kind of a frumpy girl, but not uncute, with a frame that's both scrawny and chubby (which could perhaps be my miracle if the Church ever beatifies me: "St. Gabriela, it is Said, was Blessede by the Lorde to be both Scrawnye and Chubbye").

My curly brown hair is a mix of my dad's dark, wiry curls and my mom's wavy, blond locks. I've got light brown skin and a handful of freckles across my nose.

The mailboxes are set into a massive iron rectangle, as old as the building itself. I retrieve apartment 305's mail from its keyed cubby and proceed to the elevator, which is also as old as the building. It's the kind that has an iron accordion gate you pull back. When the car arrives, I enter and select floor three. I leaf idly through the stack of mail as the room glides up. There's a bank statement and an ad for a sporting goods store. The gas bill. A dumb magazine Dad reads called *Fiscal Frontrunners*. Then there is one more letter.

The elevator dings. The doors open.

They wait.

They close.

I'm still inside, staring at the final envelope. It's light red. There's no stamp on it, no return address, and no address for the recipient. There's only a first name. My name.

It's a Death Letter.

The elevator begins to descend—someone has called it back to the lobby. Quickly, I cover the letter in the other mail, so when the doors open on the ground floor I appear to Mr. Sanders to be absorbed in a deep (though unlikely) meditation on closeout golf cleats. I step out and he steps in.

I return outside and start walking. Dad's magazine and the other mail falls through my fingers, and I grip the letter tight, crumpling it a little, thinking that it cannot be there. Not for me. I'm in a daze. I take a left turn and a right turn, moving absently, my mind possessed with a static turbulence, like boiling water.

I find myself standing outside of St. Mary's, my church. It's a long building with a humble steeple, stretching for half the block. I enter through the double doors. I dip my fingers in the baptismal font and cross myself, then proceed along the dark nave, structured in even rows of pews. The church is hung with somber banners, quotes about remembrance, mortality, repentance—the sober mist of Lent has begun already to descend here, though it doesn't start until next week. There are a few people inside, widely dispersed, all deep in prayer, heads bowed. No one notices me.

I slide into an empty pew, lay down my book bag, and hold the red letter before me. Hands shaking, I quietly tear it open and remove a single sheet of rose-colored paper and a rose-colored return envelope with the name HERCULE typed on it. The letter is only a few lines long, but for a moment I can't read it. My brain rejects the alphabet. I see shapes, but they are hieroglyphs—not even hieroglyphs: bugs. I focus my eyes with a great act of will, and run them over the words.

Dear Gabriela,
You've been chosen for departure. How about next Wednesday? That gives you a week. Save a dance for me.
— *Hercule*

There are tears on my cheeks, which leaked out without me noticing. I dry my eyes on my sleeve, then stand and pull my book bag over my shoulder. I exit the church and head home.

breaking the news

The Rivera living room, by my mom's decree, is spare and well-kept, representative of what she does for a living (interior design consultation for Lockton's Department Store). There's a blue vinyl couch, a long, narrow coffee table, and two bentwood chairs. A small stand holds the telephone and telephone directory.

The rest of the place is cluttered with Dad's stuff, which, though various, is invariable in its oldness. The dining room table, visible from the entryway as I open the front door, is piled with (among other things) a yellowed folio of newspapers, the PQR volume of an out-of-print genealogical encyclopedia, and a brick of cellophane-sealed greeting cards tied with a faded vellum bow. On the floor adjacent there's a group of office boxes labeled DEACC JAN, DEACC FEB, and DEACC MAR. Dad works for the Municipal Archives, and he loves his work, often rescuing things that the archives is getting rid of.

Mom and Dad are in the living room as I enter. Dad is standing, holding the telephone receiver to his ear. He's wearing his work clothes: brown pants and a brown suit jacket on top of a blue shirt and a wide black tie, which curves over his ample belly. His long, curly hair is held in a gray-streaked ponytail. He looks angry, and this set of his features only increases when he sees me. He says roughly into the phone, "Never mind, she just walked in." He hangs up, glaring.

Mom is sitting on the couch, legs crossed, one pale arm slung casually over the back. She's less prone to worry than Dad, though they keep a united front when it comes to my whereabouts. She looks coolly at me and pushes a long strand of blond hair behind one ear, as if readying that ear to receive the explanation for my lateness.

For a second, I'm not sure what I'm going to do. I open my mouth hesitantly, and then, with the force of a ruptured water main, I cry out. I fall to the floor, my book bag opens, and books and papers fan out across the rug.

Dad rushes to me. He kneels and places his hands on my shuddering back, his anger vanished in an instant. Mom is right behind him.

"Gabriela . . . ?" she says.

I try to collect my wits, but I can't. Still sobbing, I hold out the letter.

Dad sits heavily next to me on the floor when he sees it. He opens the rose-colored page. After a long pause, he says, *"Oh."* His tone is the one he uses for when someone points out something he's overlooked, like *"Oh,* I didn't know we had an unopened jar of red pepper flakes in the pantry." After another pause he says, "This is some kind of . . ." The last word here would be *joke,* but he knows it's not a joke. He begins again: "There must be a . . ." He stops before saying *mistake.*

Slowly, silently, we move from the floor to the couch. My mom's shoulders start to shake. She says, "Hm, hm, hm," crying and shrugging.

"I want to keep going to school," I say. When kids like myself are chosen for departure, they can decide if they want to continue their education or leave off. I'm surprised I have the presence of mind to discuss this right now.

"We'll get you a Pardon," says Mom, reading my thoughts. "Write and ask!" Her tone is a little angry, and I can't tell if it's anger at Hercule, my Death, for sending the letter or at me for receiving it.

"Demand one!" says Dad, wiping his nose on his sleeve.

"You can't *demand* a Pardon," says Mom.

"Well, you can't *ask* for one either," says Dad. They're both right: you can't demand, and you can't ask. There's only one way to get a Pardon. You've got to be tricky.

After a quiet dinner of canned soup, we end up watching TV in the living room. It's easier than talking about the only thing we have to talk about right now, but just barely. The news is bad. War is coming—the fact of the draft is enough to convince just about anyone, and speculation focuses not on *if,* but on *when.* Some think we could begin within months, such is the speed of mobilization. It seems awfully fast (and yet, I may be long gone by then).

Eventually I go to my room, assuring Mom and Dad that I'll come out if I need anything. I leave them sitting on opposite sides of the couch, still suffering the insubstantial anger with each other that they initiated with their sharp words over my Pardon. But I see Dad starting to move toward Mom as I exit. They need comfort right now more than they need to be correct.

I close my bedroom door and sit quietly at my desk. I kick off my sneakers. Normally on a night like this I'd be stressed about school. But I don't have to do homework anymore. I drag my gaze up to my wall calendar. I put a finger on today's date: Wednesday, March third. I examine the squares following, counting down silently to myself. *Six, five, four* . . . I land finally on next Wednesday. That box is labeled ASH WEDNESDAY, the beginning of Lent. My hand trembles.

I pry my eyes away, and they move on to the only other pieces of décor on my desk: two grainy, black-and-white portraits. I've had these for as long as I can remember. The photo on the left is of a young Latino man wearing a U.S. Army uniform. This is my grandfather Gonzalo. Sometimes when I'm under a lot of stress, looking at this photo calms me. Gonzalo has a sensitive, open expression, and I think he was probably a kind man. He has my father's slightly pocked dark skin, and there's a hint of a smile around his lips. The photo was taken shortly before he left for Africa. It's a very noble image. Gonzalo's eyes are looking ahead. He knows he's doing the right thing. I feel patriotic when I look at this picture. In fact, for years patriotism was the only feeling it evoked in me. I remember as a kid making up different stories about Gonzalo. Some of them, to think back on it, were kind of gruesome. One I remember, probably based on a movie, was Gonzalo saving his buddies by jumping on a hand grenade. I used to tell these stories to my grandmother, much to my parents' chagrin. But Abuela liked them. She would say, "Yes, that's Gonzalo," verifying that my tales caught the spirit of the man: risking life and limb to carry an injured soldier back from enemy lines, giving away his last meal to a refugee, fighting bravely on while others panicked and fled.

As I got older, and I kept looking at his picture on my desk, I started to notice something that I'd missed before — Gonzalo's eyes in this photo are aglow with a deep and subtle amusement. I see a similar twinkle in my dad's eyes sometimes, and in my own. It runs through all of us Riveras. Gonzalo thought it was a little funny to get this portrait taken, so reeking with nobility. Of course he had no idea that he'd disappear within two weeks of leaving for Tunisia, never to be heard from again. If he'd received a letter to that effect in advance, I wonder if his eyes would sparkle so.

The other photo on my desk is of an elegant white couple. They're dressed expensively, the woman with a jeweled necklace and the man with glinting diamond cuff links. They're in their thirties, both smiling, but their eyes don't sparkle like Gonzalo's. The man, who could be called dashing except for the cruel bent of his eyebrows, looks imperiously at the camera. The woman glances disinterestedly to one side. These are my mother's parents, the Mason-Hunts. I'm fascinated by this picture because I'm repelled by it. These two are still alive somewhere, as far as I know. I've never met them. They objected to Mom's marriage to Dad and disowned her. I guess they said all kinds of things about Dad's "values" and the "kind of people" he came from — the regular euphemisms for being brown.

It's weird to think that I'm the physical embodiment of an idea these two found so distasteful. The very person I am — my hair, my skin, my eyes. Somewhere, wherever they are, the Mason-Hunts wish they could have prevented my birth. I guess they'll probably never know about my Death Letter. If they did, though, I wonder — would they be pleased? Would they feel somehow vindicated?

The clear difference between these photos often helps me orient myself, and with a last look at the nobility and humor of

Gonzalo's eyes, I pull a blank sheet from my desk drawer. At the top I write "Wrap-Up List."

Every kid learns about Wrap-Up Lists in school: a person's attempt to organize what they want to finish before their time runs out. The list is sent to the attending Death, who renders Influence — which is sometimes supernatural and other times merely advisory.

The image suggested by the term *Wrap-Up List* implies that you have things to wrap — your lifetime of pursuits and accomplishments. But I'm barely sixteen. I'm still more or less in my original container. Nonetheless, I start writing out some ideas. I throw them onto the page quickly, without much thought. "Millionaire," I scrawl. "Famous. First kiss." As these appear, they produce an effect I hadn't anticipated. I feel . . . even worse. The list is stupid. Writing "First kiss" imparts a swift and awful sense of hopelessness, and when I follow it with "Make the cheer squad," I drop the pen to the desktop.

At the very moment I'm confronted with this painful missive from my own interior, I'm rescued by a knock on my bedroom door.

"Come in!" I say, relieved.

Dad enters, his big shoulders bulking through. "Sorry to disturb you, Gabby," he says, frowning as he remembers that I've forbidden him to call me that (since I started high school last year).

"It's okay, Dad."

"I just phoned St. Mary's." (He says the name of our church like you'd say *S'Mores:* S'Mary's.) "I talked to Father Ernesto. He's there if you'd like to see him."

"Now?" I say.

"Yes."

I stand, folding my poor list and sliding it into my pocket. "Let's go," I say.

It's typical to consult with a priest when something important happens — just to get some perspective. Maybe a non-Catholic would go to a counselor, or a psychotherapist. My family goes to Father Ernesto. I don't know how much I believe in the doctrines of my religion — I'm neither here nor there on a lot of it, and if my mood was a little different at present I'd probably be angry at Dad for his presumption. But because I'm scared, I'm glad.

Dad's car is a big old station wagon with wood paneling. It's dusty and worn, and the back seats and hatchback trunk are filled to the ceiling with boxes — stuff Dad has rescued from the Municipal Archives. He can't bring himself to get rid of any of it, but Mom won't allow it in the apartment either.

We don't really need to drive to St. Mary's — it's only a few blocks away — but I don't mind. I crack my window as the car picks up speed and the cool springtime air rushes in. I'm hoping for the scent of the flowers I smelled earlier, but no luck.

Shortly, we pull into the parking lot between the church

and the rectory. The church is long, low, and obscure at night, its steeple grazed by two bluish lights shining from the roof. The rectory is an inviting building next door, an old two-story farmhouse with a lit gravel walk to the front porch. Dad rings the bell, which plays the opening bars of "Let All Mortal Flesh Keep Silence." An instant later, the door opens.

"Welcome, Riveras! Please come in," says Father Ernesto, his accent thick, his voice friendly. He's a large man who moves with a slow dignity that always has impressed me (even after I learned that it's the result of knee problems). He's clean-shaven, with an aged, rectangular face capable of expressing everything from gleeful solicitousness to mortal strictness. He's wearing his priest's collar and a dark suit, obviously expecting our visit. We follow him slowly past the stairwell that ascends to his and Father Salerno's apartments, and we enter a sitting room where the fireplace burns low, with three chairs gathered before it.

We sit. The fire crackles.

"Gabriela," says Father, "I'm glad you've come on this difficult night. I would like to know what I can do, personally, for you. You know that your family is very special to me."

I do know this. Father Ernesto is the priest who married Gonzalo and Abuela. He also married my parents, and oversaw Mom's conversion to the church. He baptized and confirmed me. His face is a monument, and his words a benevolent force.

"I was working on my Wrap-Up List," I say.

"I'm glad," says Father Ernesto. "It's a blessing."

"I don't know if I think so," I say. (When I was in Confirmation classes I was the one kid who ever challenged Father Ernesto, and he liked me for it. It's because of that, in fact, that I have any faith at all—Father was a good example to me that religion didn't have to replace thoughtfulness.)

"All things made by God can be blessings," he says now, an easy parry. "Of course it isn't always so simple," he adds.

"Yeah, it's just . . ." I say. I fall silent, embarrassed.

Father turns to my dad. "Señor Rivera," he says, "could Gabriela and I have a moment alone?" Without a word, Dad stands and exits smoothly, closing the front door behind him as he steps out onto the porch.

I unfold in my chair enough to pull my Wrap-Up List out of my jeans pocket. I grit my teeth, and through that reluctant gate recite: "Millionaire. Famous. First kiss." The words squeak through. Fortunately, Father Ernesto stops me before I have to say "Make the cheer squad."

"Gabriela," he says, "I see you making an unhappy expression."

"Yeah," I sigh.

"Do you remember when in Confirmation class we discussed the guiding statement St. Mary's had chosen?"

"'Spirit of Service,'" I say. It was a big deal two years ago when the church chose that motto. And kids had made fun of it because it's also the slogan of a nearby gas station. It seemed emblematic of how out of touch the church was. But right now it doesn't seem funny.

"And the verse we chose, to remind us?"

"'Each of you should use whatever gift you have received to serve others,'" I quote.

"Perhaps it's worth considering, as you create your list," says Father Ernesto.

"You're right, Father," I say.

"I'll add one thing more, also, Gabriela. I know your family holds your grandfather in high esteem, and rightly so. Think of his sacrifice, too — that he gave his own life to ensure the safety of his family, his descendants." It's funny that I was just looking at Gonzalo's picture but somehow needed this pointed out to me.

Dad and I have a quiet drive back home. He doesn't ask me what Father Ernesto said to me, and I don't volunteer. It's always been so. Dad has a respect for the Church that borders on fear. Tonight, the silence between us isn't awkward — I'm too occupied with my own thoughts. I'm imagining better items for my list. I'm thinking about *Heal the Sick* and also *Money for Church Expansion* (because I know St. Mary's wants to remodel the sanctuary). I consider *Win the War.*

Back home, Mom has made some dessert — strawberries and cream — but I don't want any. I've got work to do. I return to my room, leaving my parents figuring out if they're still mad at each other, I expect—if they can even remember what they were arguing about before. (I've learned that this isn't a necessary component of their disagreements. They have great faith in their annoyance even when they can't recall its origin.)

I close my bedroom door, sit at my desk, and open my list before me. I cross out every item I'd previously written. I'm feeling better. Before I begin again, though, I take another look at Gonzalo's portrait, thinking about what Father Ernesto said. It's true, my grandfather made a heroic decision. I look into his noble, distant gaze . . .

But there is that gleam in his eyes. That tricky amusement, which has nothing to do with nobility. I don't know what it is, but it makes me want to smile. "Spirit of Service," I say to Gonzalo, and then: "Free Wash and Wax with Every Oil Change!"

At that moment, a waft of spring air blows through my window, carrying with it that scent—the bracing and rich smell of flowers that sends my heart fluttering hopefully.

Now, I think, glancing over the crossed-out items of my original list. One item sticks out: First kiss, I had written. I write it again now, at the top of my new list, but a little different:

1. First Kiss—for Iris

The words appear as by divine inspiration. I glance at Gonzalo. His eyes sparkle. He's laughing. *Spirit of Service!*

I imagine my Death, Hercule, getting my Wrap-Up List and seeing this item. I smile wider. I move my pen to the next line down and write: "2. First Kiss — for Raahi." This is followed quickly by "3. First Kiss — for Sarena." (She could probably use one, too, since I'm handing them out.)

I let out an unexpected snort, which I do sometimes by accident when something's funnier than I thought it'd be. I clap a hand over my mouth. I wonder if Father Ernesto would approve . . .

Then I write, "4. First kiss — for me, from Sylvester." I feel I've earned it, after generously supplying these other kisses. Who would begrudge me?

I round out the list with a final item. This appears on almost every Wrap-Up List that has ever been created. I pen it quickly, although it's the most important thing on the whole piece of paper:

5. *Pardon*

A Pardon means, "You can go back home, Gabriela, and live the rest of your life as if none of this ever happened." Deaths never give these out willingly, though. Granting a Pardon is some kind of misfortune for them. If a Death gives a Pardon, that Death disappears — for fifty years at least, sometimes forever.

But you can manage it if you're smart. Every Death has

what's called a Noble Weakness. This is a good deed that, if you accomplish it, forces them to let you go. They conceal this Noble Weakness with great care, and guessing it is difficult because it could be almost anything. If you ask for a Pardon on your Wrap-Up List, your Death will give you a Hint. Solve the Hint and accomplish the correct Deed, and you'll be Pardoned.

It almost never happens.

I look over my list. I've heard of people with hundreds of items, but it's said that Deaths don't like long lists. This is enough, anyway, and I'm still amused about Hercule reading it. Having to exert his precious Influence for the sake of a bunch of kisses!

1. First Kiss — for Iris
2. First Kiss — for Raahi
3. First Kiss — for Sarena
4. First Kiss — for me, from Sylvester
5. Pardon

I spare another glance at Gonzalo, whose eyes glint approvingly. The Mason-Hunts, for their part, seem to neither approve nor disapprove. As usual, I can't convince myself that they'd care what I do. They look right through me.

I jot a copy of the list for myself and seal the original into Hercule's rose return envelope. I leave the apartment quietly, walk the hall, and step into the elevator. As I descend, I experience an unexpected memory from last year. I don't know why it hits me at this moment, but my brain is very insistent.

It's the memory of me entering Central High for the first time, freshman year. I was looking for my homeroom, thinking I'd never find my way — not because I was lost but because it seemed like there was nowhere to get to. The place was full of people, but to me it felt lonesome, alien — purposeless. I was caught totally off-guard by this.

My junior high had been a small school full of kids from St. Mary's, but Central High wasn't where my onetime Sunday school cohorts ended up. Due to district dividing lines, I became a Central High Cougar instead of a South High Jaguar. Every face I saw that morning was unknown to me.

My debut report card that year was almost straight Fs. I was put on academic probation and sent to Ms. Lime, the school's most pear-shaped English instructor (since hers was the only class I was passing). At our first meeting, Ms. Lime asked me, "What are your goals, Gabriela?"

I said I didn't have any. It was true — with no place to be, and no place to go, how could I have goals? "I feel like I'm in limbo," I said. Ms. Lime took the term in the popular sense, not being Catholic, but I intended its ecclesiastical meaning — the place, neither heaven nor hell, where unbaptized babies go. Limbo is not like purgatory. In purgatory, you have a purpose — to cleanse your soul so you can get to heaven.

Limbo is a permanent state, with neither the risk of damnation nor the possibility of salvation. A tractionless finale.

Ms. Lime, despite her limited acquaintance with the doctrine, offered me some good advice. "You need goals," she said. We laid out a sheet, and she wrote "Gabriela's Goals" at the top. I remember staring at the name: Gabriela. I'd always been Gabby before, but now I found myself transformed. I saw the first possibility of my situation — that I was on the verge of becoming someone new.

It wasn't easy at first. "Gabriela's Goals" seemed empty, fake, like a paper house that would never keep out the weather. But I applied myself, and the goals Ms. Lime and I placed on that sheet solidified. My new name became my real name. Over the course of the next several months, I made some friends and improved my grades (two of my goals). I worked my way off of academic probation. At my last meeting with Ms. Lime, she told me she was proud of me. "You had a shock this year," she said. "Life was bigger and colder than you thought. But you've made your direction. You're on your way."

Now, as the reminiscence ends, I feel the cold blow back in as strongly as I've ever felt it. I see my little life amid a void — weightless, directionless, infinite. All victories in such a kingdom are won in vain. All castles are paper.

I drop my letter into the rigid mouth of the outgoing mail slot, and the awful chill passes through me as if I were nothing.

six days before
departure day

the announcement

The following morning, I arrive in Ms. Lime's English class as the opening bell sounds. Behind me is Wendy Overton, who leans toward me anxiously as I sit and hisses, *"Pop quiz!"*

Wendy is one of those kids who seem able to do almost anything. She's a short, slightly stocky girl, who some days looks almost like a guy — but when she comes to school dressed in her cheer uniform (like today), she's the picture of cuteness. She enjoys the distinction of being the only member of the cheer squad both small enough to get thrown into the air *and* strong enough to throw other cheerleaders into the air (both a *flyer* and a *base*, in parlance). Additionally, she's the only cheerleader who's also in the marching band — she plays flute. But every superhuman creature has a weakness, and Wendy's is English. I often let her cheat off of my quizzes, because I like her — even though I'm also a little jealous of her (I tried out for cheer squad last year and didn't make it). This morning, though, I don't respond to her at all. I just stare straight ahead.

Iris enters. "Hi, Wendy, how's it going?" she says, pausing behind me.

"Pop quiz," says Wendy, very focused.

Iris sits next to me and lays a hand on my desk to get my attention. She wants to tell me what happened yesterday with the Singing Man. When I don't look over at her, she says, "Gabriela? You okay?"

The intercom at the front of the room crackles to life, and Principal Kreisler's nasal voice sounds through the old speaker. "Hello, Cougars. It's Thursday, March fourth. Hamburgers and tater tots. Put Sunday night's game on your calendar, playoff against the South High Jaguars, seven p.m. (Go Cougs), and please attend the varsity fundraiser in the parking lot after school today — dunk tank with starting receiver Sylvester Hale. Lastly, on a sad note, Gabriela Rivera has been selected for departure. Please offer your condolences." The intercom clicks off.

The whole class turns to look at me with a collective gasp of disbelief. I knew this was coming — I had Mom call it in, thinking I'd get it over all at once.

"Gabriela!" Ms. Lime exclaims, shocked.

Iris is standing next to me — she has jumped out of her chair.

Ms. Lime delays the pop quiz and initiates a peer discussion session on the reading, during which some kids approach me as Principal Kreisler recommended, and offer condolences.

I turn to Iris. "Want to skip?" I ask.

Everyone's eyes are on me as we go.

We walk toward the Marking Street Café, which is Iris's favorite coffee shop. I've never liked it. It's where the Deaths usually go to get coffee, and Iris has always been fascinated with them. She never passes up a chance to see one or two.

When we arrive there's a line of middle-aged business-people waiting to place orders, and one Death among them, a good three feet taller than everyone else. His head nearly brushes the ceiling. His straight gray hair floats in broad curves around his shoulders, and his silvery sharkskin suit glimmers. Iris leans toward me and whispers, "Greeley." I'm sure she doesn't know them all, but she knows a lot of them. Greeley orders coffee and disappears out the door, aquatic and slow, while we're still in line.

Iris and I get a pot of black tea to share and find a table by the window. Once we're seated, she says, "Gabriela, what the *hell?*" She slaps the tabletop with one hand. "Is this for *real?*"

I produce Hercule's letter and pass it to her.

"Oh, I can't *believe* it," she says.

As she reads, I pour us each a cup of tea. "Have you ever heard of Hercule?" I ask.

"No. This letter is awful, by the way — what an ass! 'Save a dance for me.'" I know what her next question will be. Before she asks, I produce the copy I made of my Wrap-Up List. I hesitate for a moment out of embarrassment, but finally hand it over. She's my best friend, after all.

She looks it over soberly, and her expression changes from deep concern to what I might call scandalized admiration.

"This?" she says, shaking the list. *"This?"*

"Yeah," I say.

"You *mailed* this? To your *Death?*" She continues rattling the page.

"That's right," I say.

"Gabriela, I can't *believe* you!" Her eyes sparkle, and I can tell she's thrilled with it. She laughs. "I shouldn't be surprised!"

"What do you mean?" I say.

"Well, it's just . . . you're just . . ." She tries to find the words, but there is apparently no term for the thing I am. She lays the list the table and puts one red nail on the first item. "So, you think I need a first kiss?"

"Um, maybe?"

"All right, I probably do," she says, obviously touched to find herself on the page.

Then we're interrupted by voices: "Gabriela! *Gabriela!*" Sarena and Raahi rush through the café door, past the line, to our table.

"The announcement — " says Sarena.

"We heard — " says Raahi, close behind.

"Is it true?" they say in unison.

My expression tells the tale.

Sarena says, "I can't believe it! Did you get a date?"

"Next Wednesday," I say.

"A week?" says Raahi.

"This . . . this is just *stupid!*" says Sarena. She brushes her braids back with an annoyed flick of her wrist. They both seem angry, like my parents did last night. "You've got to get a *Pardon!*" she says.

"That's right," says Iris. "We have no time to lose."

Sarena and Raahi grab chairs and sit on either side of me, and we all look to Iris. She's been interested in this stuff since forever. She knows more about the Deaths, more about departure, more about getting Pardons, than just about anyone. "The first step is already complete," she says. "Gabriela sent her Wrap-Up List to Hercule. When we get his reply, we can start doing research."

"We have to find his Noble Weakness, right?" says Raahi.

"Right," says Iris. "And Gabriela has to accomplish it."

"And his weakness can be *anything?*" says Sarena.

Iris rolls her eyes. "Our schools are failing us," she laments. It's true we don't learn much about all of this at school, but it's understandable. Departures are only one percent of all fatalities, after all. "Hercule's Noble Weakness will be a significant act relating to *generosity*. It won't be small, like baking someone a birthday cake. It will require a lot of you, Gabriela."

"Like jumping on a hand grenade," I say.

"Sort of," says Iris. "It could have to do with putting yourself in danger to save someone's life. But don't get yourself killed — you can't use a Pardon if you're dead."

"What if you never have an opportunity to save someone's life?" says Raahi.

"Well, you can promise to do it," says Iris.

"That counts?" says Sarena.

"Promises count if you really mean them," says Iris. "Deaths can tell the attitude of your heart, though — if you don't mean it, it won't work."

"I'd jump on a hand grenade to save your life, Iris," I say.

"But would you *really*, Gabriela? Think it over."

"I really would," I say. "You're my best friend! Nothing's going to come along to change that."

Iris narrows her eyes, and there's something in her gaze — an intensity that's so focused it makes me a little uncomfortable, and I look away. Iris continues. "The Noble Weakness could relate to almost anything. Maybe giving your time — nursing a sick person, for instance. Or giving up your space — inviting someone to live with you. It could even be giving up possessions. Some are very specific, and some are more general. There's no telling. We'll have to wait for the Hint."

After spending a few hours in further speculation and several cups of coffee, we return to school in the afternoon to watch a little of the dunk tank fundraiser for the football team. The spectacle is in full swing when we arrive. Students swarm around the tank, chatting in groups, watching, some lined up to take a shot. I notice Sylvester Hale's dad standing near the edge of the crowd, talking with one of the assistant coaches. Mr. Hale is a big booster for the football team, and he's easy to spot not only because of his gleaming, bald head, but because he has only one arm. The other he lost, I gather, in the military, though I don't know the story of it. I've always steered clear of the man. He gets really angry sometimes, and I even saw him forcibly removed from a football game once after he stormed onto the field in a rage. At the moment, he's not really doing anything. Just chatting with people.

Finally my eyes land on Sylvester, the star of the event, poised over the water on his collapsible seat. He's slouched, casual, hands on his knees. No one has dunked him yet. His hair is rakish, and his skin curves generously over his fit frame. Every bend of him transfixes my eye. I wonder how many girls here are dreaming of him right now.

The transparent sides of the dunk tank are adorned with amusing imagery, intended, I suppose, to make the dunking process more fun. At the top of the tank, painted clouds and birds, and a smiling sun wearing sunglasses. Below the water line, a school of grinning fish, a diminutive underwater castle, and some underwater houses that resemble a regular neighborhood. I'd think they would have put a bunch of merpeople down there, or King Triton and his servants, but there's no one. The castle and houses look kind of lonely. It's as if Sylvester's about to be dumped into a ghost town.

"Wendy's next," Sarena observes. "She'll dunk him for sure." Raahi is standing next to Sarena, and I notice how much taller he is than her—maybe a foot taller. I noticed that yesterday, too, I recall, when they were walking up the hill together after school, Raahi carrying Sarena's trumpet. That seems like a thousand years ago.

"Go-o!" shouts Iris. She's not generally interested in football, but she appears enthusiastic for Wendy to hit that bull's-eye.

Coach Frank hands Wendy three blue and green beanbags stenciled with the Cougars logo. Wendy looks around at her audience. Everyone knows and respects her potential for doing just about anything (except pass English). Sylvester, a little nervous, lets fly a sudden insult: "You throw like a girl!" he says, though she has not yet thrown anything. His voice, brassy and confident, causes some good-natured laughter in the crowd.

Wendy turns to Coach Frank. She hands two of the three beanbags back to him, leaving her with only one. A hush falls over us all as she steps to the chalk line on the ground. She eyes the target. Then she carefully pitches her single beanbag underhand—throwing like a girl! It arcs gracefully straight to the target and strikes it dead-on. Sylvester's seat flops, and he plunges into the water with a manly bellow. The crowd goes wild.

"She's so cool!" says Sarena.

"Yeah," says Iris, as I attentively watch Sylvester climb, dripping, from the plunge.

After fielding more heartfelt condolences from classmates and friends both dear and distant, I lead Iris, Sarena, and Raahi back to the apartment to see if the mail has arrived. We enter the lobby and approach the wall of mailboxes. I nervously open 305's cubby, which sings on its old hinges, and pull forth the mail. Among the junk and bills there's a red envelope, blank but for my name.

We all stare at it. I say, "Um, is anyone hungry?" I slip the envelope into my jacket pocket. "Do you guys want to come up?"

Mom and Dad are both home. "Hello, honey," says Mom casually, with a tone in her voice that makes it obvious she and Dad have been waiting for me. Furthermore, I think that neither of them went to work today. They've both been home, worrying, and they're still radiating the anger and grief they expressed last night.

Dad says to my friends, "Iris, Sarena, Raahi, it's nice to see you." My parents have hosted these three plenty of times during living room study sessions, field trips, et cetera. We've all watched scary movies together and eaten birthday cake. They've all attended the weekly Rivera Family Tuesday Night Dinner.

"Did you pick up the mail, Gabriela?" Mom asks.

I place the stack on the coffee table. "Hercule wrote back, but I haven't opened it yet," I say. Fortunately, everyone is understanding about my reluctance.

While my parents assemble chicken tacos, my friends and I clear the dining room table, which is covered with some of Dad's recent acquisitions from the archives. There's a blue box labeled BUREAU OF TOURISM (which Raahi takes to the hall closet and places atop three other boxes similarly labeled), a stack of old record sleeves tied into a block with twine (which Sarena stashes in the corner next to a historic set of regional memoirs), and a metal tin that opens to reveal some unused Yosemite-themed postcards (which I put on the desk in Dad's study). We finish just as my parents enter with tacos and bowls of reheated pozole. Our plates are massive antique disks painted with peacocks, which belonged to Mom's parents, the Mason-Hunts.

"Let's pray," says Dad. We all fold our hands obediently. Dad is the leader of a prayer group at church and often says the closing prayer there. Unlike most people I've known who pray publicly, Dad is always brief. ("If Jesus was truly a man," he told me once, "then He can be bored.") "Dear Lord Jesus," he prays, "thank you for this food, and the knowledge to prepare it. Thank you for bringing Raahi, Sarena, and Iris here this evening as we try to understand your will and live in accordance with your wishes. Amen."

"Amen," I echo.

. . .

After dinner, Raahi and Sarena both have to go. Sarena has sound check with the Washington Fifteen at the Caballero, and Raahi told his mom he'd be home — she's anxious after him, since he's leaving for basic training early next Tuesday. (Raahi's mom, Charvi, is an amazing woman. She's a senior officer for an American corporation with business interests in India. She's extremely tough, independent, intelligent, and according to Raahi, worried about him and wanting him home for dinner.)

Iris and I clear the table. I see Dad about to give me a reprieve from my chores, but he stops himself. I imagine him thinking, "Maybe Gabriela should do her chores, to enjoy the normality of them." I feel bad. It's hard for me, sure, to have found out I have only a handful of days left, but it may be harder in some ways for my parents. They've known me longer than I have.

While I wash the dishes and enjoy the normality, Iris calls her parents to tell them she's going to spend the night here. She hands me the phone so I can talk to her dad, which is awkward, but Mr. Van Voorhees just wants me to know how sorry he is to hear the news. He passes the phone to Mrs. Van Voorhees, and she says the same.

Then, finally, Iris and I go to my room. To look at the letter my Death has sent me.

hints

Deaths are tricksters. They never give a straight answer about anything. Instead of sending answers, Deaths send Hints.

I sit at my desk, and Iris settles onto the edge of my bed, feet dangling. She kicks off her shoes as I tear open the letter, and shoes and envelope fall to the carpet. I unfold the page. There's no "Dear Gabriela" this time — it's just my original handwritten list, with Hercule's annotations scribbled below.

1. First Kiss — for Iris
— A cavalier request, Gabriela.
2. First Kiss — for Raahi
— See #1.
3. First Kiss — for Sarena
— See #1.

4. First Kiss — for me, from Sylvester
— A bedroom for books.
— The Fields.
5. Pardon
— Always about to disappear.

"Are these *Hints?*" I say. They don't look like Hints.

"They are," says Iris.

Numbers 1, 2, and 3 seem like a chastisement. Maybe I *was* being cavalier. I don't know. It's not every day you find out you've got a week to live. "'A bedroom for books,'" I muse. "Shelf? Bookcase?" I feel Iris's eyes boring into me, and I meet her gaze. "What?" I say.

"Do you feel it?" she asks.

"Feel what?"

"The *Influence,*" she says. "As soon as you opened this, Hercule started helping you."

"I don't feel anything," I say. I focus on the Hints, and suddenly the solution to the first line of Number 4 jumps out, like a fish leaping into a boat. "Got it!" I say, surprised.

"What? Which one?"

"'A bedroom for books'! Where are all of our books right now?" I say.

"In our bags?"

"Not a bag — a *room. Lockers.* Our lockers at school."

"Maybe there's something in your locker," says Iris.

"A love note?" I laugh. It's improbable, but now that I have the magical aid of my Death, who knows? "Funny to think," I say. "Normally I go to my locker every day, but if this Hint hadn't appeared . . ."

"You might never have gone back there, after getting your Death Letter," says Iris.

After this, we divvy my desk into halves so Iris can do homework while I keep figuring. The minutes pass, and my early success fades. The other Hints prove impenetrable. Next to me, Iris scrawls formulas for her chemistry class, but she keeps peeking at my list, obviously more interested in helping me than in calculating molecular weights.

Eventually, our energies flag. It's gotten late. I lend Iris a pair of flannel pajamas, and while she puts them on, I go say good night to Mom and Dad in the living room. I bring my Wrap-Up List with me, thinking I'll show them Hercule's Hints, but by the time I've reached the couch where they're sitting together watching TV, I've changed my mind. I'm not sure why. I've folded the list in half and am holding it by my side, nearly out of sight. Maybe I'm embarrassed that I'm going to depart in the first place. I'm not sure.

"Good night," I say, even as their twin gazes flick back and forth between my face and the folded list.

"The Hints," says Dad, gesturing at the paper. "Could we see them, Gabby?"

"Gabriela," says Mom, "maybe we can help."

"Er, not right now, okay?" I say. I crumple the folded sheet, trying to wish it into a pocket I don't have.

"Then *when?*" says Dad.

"Maybe tomorrow . . ." I say.

"Maybe?" Dad echoes. "Gabriela, your mother and I want to help you."

I really wish I had a pocket. Why don't pajamas have pockets? The list seems to be getting bigger, and maybe glowing, and beeping.

Then, out of nowhere, Dad's hand flicks out—he grabs it from me.

My eyes grow large with surprise. Dad is not that kind of guy. He's someone who discusses; who talks it out with you; who, maybe, issues ultimatums. He would never—

But he has. Before he can even glance at the sheet, my own hand leaps. I grab the list back from him, and an angry stalemate of stern glares follows.

"Gabriela!" says Mom, loudly, and her tone speaks volumes. It says, *I am going to severely chastise your father after you leave the room because that was uncalled for. However, the fault is partly yours, and you should apologize now so we don't all go to bed angry.*

I'm flushed and outraged, but she's right. "I'm sorry, Dad," I say. "But—you have to respect me."

Dad glowers.

"We both want to help, Gabriela," says Mom. "But we'll wait until you decide it's time."

"Good night," I say.

"Good night," says Mom.

"Good night, Gabriela," says Dad. "I'm sorry."

"Let's forget it," I say. I pause, and then smile. "That's *final*," I add. Saying "That's final" to Dad is kind of a joke. He says it sometimes when he doesn't want to entertain further discussion.

He blanches when I say it now, but then sees the humor in it. He snorts suddenly, just like I do when something strikes me funny. "Okay," he says. "Don't forget your rosary," he adds.

"I won't."

"What would you like for breakfast tomorrow?"

"Maybe . . . chicken fajitas?"

"No maybes," says Dad. "Chicken fajitas is *final*."

As I retreat down the hall, I hear Mom's intense and quiet voice as she begins to tell Dad off. I wish she wouldn't, even though he deserves it. I just don't want anyone arguing right now.

Back in my room, I find Iris changed into her borrowed PJs.

"I have to say my rosary really quick," I tell her, going to my desk.

She's seen me do it plenty of times. As she gets under the covers, I take out my set of plastic beads. I place the cross between thumb and forefinger and begin, silently—the Apostles' Creed, the Our Father, a handful of Hail Marys and the Doxology get me past the introductory block to the first Mystery. On Thursdays I usually pray the Luminous Mysteries. The first is the baptism of Christ, when the heavens open and the Spirit of God descends like a dove. It's normally a comforting image — up there in heaven, something like a dove — but tonight I imagine old pigeons waddling in gutters, bobbing heads, rigid pinkish toes, twitchy red-rimmed eyes. I look down at the plastic loop in my lap. The cross looks like a bird foot.

I return the rosary to my desk, flip off the lights, and climb into bed next to Iris. You know how you can tell, in the darkness, if someone's eyes are open? I've always found that strange.

"That was fast," says Iris.

"I couldn't finish," I say.

There's a rustling under the covers, and Iris's hand finds mine. "We'll figure this out, Gabriela," she says. "We'll start research tomorrow. We can go to the archives after school."

"Once we find out Hercule's Noble Weakness, then what?"

"Then you'll perform it, or sincerely promise to. Finally, in the Fields, right before you cross under the Oaks, you tell Hercule that you did it. He'll Pardon you, and you'll walk back home."

"Naked," I say.

"Right," says Iris. (That's a well-known thing about people who get Pardons—it's as if they came so close to their end that they lost even their clothes.) "Don't worry, though," she adds. "I'll bring an extra dress and meet you on the way back. I don't want you to be cold."

The covers rustle again. Iris turns toward me and puts her arms around me. We're both shivering.

five days before
departure day

bedroom for books

The next morning is Friday. Mom, Dad, Iris, and I eat a brief, early breakfast of chicken fajitas. It looks like Mom and Dad are both planning to go to work today. Dad's in his brown suit, and Mom is wearing her slacks. We eat quietly, and neither they nor I bring up Hercule's Hints. I mention to Dad that Iris and I will stop by the archives after school, and I can tell he's glad.

Iris and I are both curious what I'll find in my locker today, but she heads to Ms. Lime's room once we arrive at school, to give me a little privacy. I walk the busy hall, lined with uniform gray doors. I reach mine, twirl in the combination, and find my books within, looking well-rested.

A scrap of paper washes out and slips to the ground. Such is the rush before first period that three passersby step on it before I can pick it up. When I finally get it in hand, I see that it's a note.

meet me at the 45th street canal. noon saturday — sylvester

My eyes widen. It's the height of unlikelihood, and I begin to understand what Iris was talking about last night when she spoke of the Influence. My mind fills with scenarios of Sylvester confessing the most improbable of crushes on me. Even the Hint that led me here, "A bedroom for books," brims with romance.

Minutes later, I take my regular seat in Ms. Lime's class between Iris and the window. Normally Wendy is behind me, but she's been unexpectedly displaced this morning by Raahi and Sarena. Raahi reaches forward and puts his hand on my shoulder.

"Hi," he says.

"Good morning!" I reply, startled to find them skipping their own classes for the sole purpose of hanging out with me here.

The bell rings, and I look to the front of the room to find that Ms. Lime is not up there. Instead, there's a soldier. He's dressed in fatigues, standing at parade rest, soberly surveying the room.

"Everyone," says Ms. Lime from her desk by the far wall, "the military is on campus today to inform us about the draft. It shouldn't take long." She turns to the soldier. "Go ahead,

Sergeant Mistletoe." The sergeant's name catches the class, and me, by surprise. I glance around. Everyone's trying to figure out if it's some kind of joke. Milo Stathopoulos, a huge linebacker on the football team, mouths the word to himself slowly (*Mis-el-tow?*), a confounded expression on his face.

But the sergeant's name tag corroborates Ms. Lime's assertion. I think, *Mistletoe! First kiss!* I turn in my seat and spot Sylvester at the back of the room, sitting with some of his buddies. He doesn't seem to notice me, though, and my excitement fades — it's silly to assume that everything that happens to me now will be the result of Hercule's Influence. The sergeant has no doubt been named Mistletoe since he was born.

"*Selective Service* is the preferred term, ma'am," says the sergeant to Ms. Lime. Then he addresses the class. "I'll make this brief, everyone," he says. His voice shakes a bit, and there's a tiny gleam of sweat at his temple. The sergeant is nervous. I wonder how old he is. His uniform is a little misleading. I think he might be in his twenties — not much older than all of us, really.

"If you have received a letter from the government conscripting you for compulsory service," he says, "compliance is mandatory. You will be assigned a doctor and receive a physical examination. You will have two weeks to put your affairs in order before reporting for active duty. I expect some of you have . . ." He trails off and turns to Ms. Lime. "Are these sophomores?" he asks. "Mostly," she replies. He continues: "I expect some of you have friends who have received draft letters.

It is very important for you to encourage them to remember that the draft was ratified by your government and signed into law by the president."

Then a voice I didn't expect to hear is raised from the back of the room. It's Sylvester. "Is there any way to volunteer *before* you get drafted?" he asks. That's a strange question.

"U.S. citizens eighteen years or older can volunteer at the downtown recruiting office," says Mistletoe.

"My birthday's next week," says Sylvester. "Can I volunteer now, just so it's on record?"

"Hey, Sylvester," says Raahi, turning in his seat, "I'll give you my draft card if you give me your birthday." Some kids laugh at this.

"No, draft cards are not transferable," says Mistletoe.

"I *want* to volunteer," says Sylvester. These words could sound challenging — a blow aimed at Raahi's patriotism — but Sylvester's tone is too earnest. "If we look strong, maybe there won't be a war."

"No, there will be," says a new voice: Iris. "It's already begun," she says. "Gabriela is proof of it."

My face grows suddenly hot, and I'm thankful my complexion isn't prone to blushing. I'm mystified about what kind of point she's trying to make, as is the rest of the class. She continues:

"Departures are always one percent of all fatalities," she says. "So when they increase, it means deaths from other causes will also increase. And departures are up *five percent* in the last six months. Five percent! That's thousands — tens of thousands — above normal."

This gives the class pause, me included. It hadn't occurred to me that my situation was attributable to anything other than bad luck. The notion that I'm part of the measurable cost of an approaching war strikes me as profoundly as a slap in the face.

Mistletoe is looking right at me. "I'm sorry to hear this, young lady," he says. And his eyes seem sad, which surprises me. Just like with Gonzalo, I'm able only with special effort to see that there's a whole person beneath the uniform. But my surprise at realizing this pales in comparison to the surprise I see in Mistletoe's own face. Because, I realize with sudden clarity, he didn't expect to feel sad either. Uniforms aren't an illusion worked only on the audience — the soldier believes it, too. As Mistletoe and I share this moment, we're both instructed. He thought, perhaps for years and certainly when he got up this morning, that when he puts on the uniform, he takes off his feelings. When he puts on the soldier, he takes off the man.

They forget themselves, I think, amazed.

"Thank you for your time today, Sergeant," says Ms. Lime, breaking the spell. "I'm sure you have other classes to visit."

"Yes, ma'am," says Mistletoe. He salutes us, the expression on his face a mixture of relief and dismay. He strides quickly out.

the archives

It's sunny after school, with a slight chilly breeze. Iris and I catch the bus out to the Municipal Archives, about a thirty-minute ride south of downtown.

The archives building was once stately, I imagine: a stone façade with granite pillars and a grand staircase leading to a pair of twenty-foot-tall double doors trimmed in brass. In later years, it turned out this wasn't such a good design, so the city started remodeling it. A wood and metal wheelchair ramp was added, partly covering the stairs. They sealed the big doors and installed an energy-efficient set of revolving ones. The windows across the front received bright white vinyl frames. The original grand idea looked good, but it didn't work. Now it's a mess, but smarter.

Iris and I, inexperienced revolving door operators, make the mistake of both entering the same compartment, and we

emerge into the lobby in a laughing tangle, to find my dad observing us from behind the front counter. "Welcome to the
Municipal Archives!" he says, brushing his shoulders in mock
officiousness.

"Hi, Dad," I say.

"Hello, Mr. Rivera," says Iris.

"I hope you two have an appointment . . . ?"

"Dad," I chide (there's a rule in the teenager handbook that
one must never be amused by parental clowning). He steps
from behind the counter, and we hug. "I laid a little ground-
work for you," he says. "These are the cards we have for
Hercule." He hands me a clipboard with a list of records loca-
tions attached. "Most are military," he says. "Hercule hasn't
generated a new record for over fifty years." As he speaks, his
levity drains.

"Thanks, Dad," I say.

"Iris knows the way down." He gestures across the room.
Iris comes here frequently to do exactly this sort of research
on various Deaths, so she leads us to the stairwell, which descends past three small landings. The natural light of the lobby
diminishes as we enter the yellow murk of the basement's fila-
ment bulbs.

"When were you last down here?" I ask.

"Couple weeks ago," says Iris. "You?"

"Sixth-grade field trip," I say.

"Really? Even though your dad works here?"

"Yeah . . ." I say, thinking, *I'm a bad daughter!* I could have stopped by, just to say hi. Maybe I could have brought him cookies. Would it have been so hard?

We reach the bottom of the stairs and enter a low-ceilinged vestibule with dark veneered walls. I glance at the clipboard and at the labels on the doorways. Straight ahead is MH 2435–4658, a typed sign with a handwritten addendum on the side reading 6707, MB7–ML07. Below that, in blue, in a different handwriting, G2.

Iris sees my confusion and holds out a hand for the clipboard. I pass it to her. She sizes it up quickly and steps toward our first objective, M6819, passing through a doorway the sign above which does not include the range containing that record. "This one would have been moved," she explains.

We travel the downward-slanting hall, the air dusty and dry. A few of the hallway bulbs have burned out, leaving dark sections that obscure some of the black-and-white photographs decorating both walls. The subjects of the photos are young soldiers in posed portraits, their uniforms perfect, their eyes confident. Not long ago, I would have been filled with patriotism to see them there, looking so handsome and brave. Now I think immediately of Sergeant Mistletoe. They forget themselves. Or they were trying to, anyway. To be the image. I've imagined myself a soldier plenty of times. And in my more recent history, I donned the short blue skirt and white gloves for cheerleader tryouts. I remember looking at myself in the locker room mirror, straightening my collar, trying to embody the spirit and image of cheerleaderishness. Trying to suppress whatever in me didn't conform to that.

I see past the uniforms in these old photos without too much difficulty. In this one, of a pale, skinny teen with curly hair as thick as wool, it's easy. He's looking down. He's remembering his life at home, everything he's about to lose. Maybe he's replaying an argument with his parents, trying to win it. The next one is easy, too — a girl dressed in a nurse's uniform. She gazes directly at the camera with a sharp wit. She's trying to see a way out. None of these kids are soldiers. There's no such thing as a soldier.

My dad and aunt always talk in reverent tones about Grandfather Gonzalo. They respect him so deeply — but they hardly knew him. I wonder what all of our lives would be like now if Gonzalo had not gone to war. What if he'd stayed home with Abuela, and raised my aunt and dad? What if he was my living grandfather now, joining us for Tuesday Night Dinner every week?

When I reach the end of the hall, I look back along the line of photos, the overhead lights flaring off the glass covers and glazing the images. Frail, confused, struggling, funny, smart, beautiful young people. They put on their uniforms and imagined they'd return in triumph, heroes.

I rush to catch up to Iris in the next room.

I find her leaning over a drawer she's pulled from a large square card catalog. It seems like she's leafing through it, but as I near her I notice she's not really doing anything. She's just standing there, staring down. I get closer and see that her eyes are closed. Her fingers are gripping the drawer tightly. I take a sudden breath, startled — it's one of those moments when you see someone's in pain but you can't tell what's causing it. I've never seen her like this before.

"Are you okay, Iris?" I say, stopping my approach a few paces off.

"Sorry," she mutters, her eyes flicking open. My words seem to have broken her trance, and she begins flipping through the cards in the drawer. She brushes an imaginary speck from her cheek.

"What's wrong?" I say.

"Nothing."

"But it *is* something." I reach out and take her wrist, pulling her from the cards. Her mouth closes tightly, and then, suddenly, she's in tears. She lunges forward and throws her arms around me. For a second I think this is about my looming departure — she's sad that she might lose her best friend. And maybe that's part of it . . . but there's more, I can tell. I put my arms around her, and she sobs quietly, her body shaking. I rub her back, not sure what to do.

Eventually, the storm passes. Iris straightens. "Well," she says. She puts one hand on the table next to the card catalog and leans on it. Obviously, I expect her to explain. She looks ruefully down at her red nails, then off into the retreating lanes of shelved records that surround us. "Gabriela," she says, more tears hovering at the edge of each word as she continues: "it was sweet of you to put my first kiss on your Wrap-Up List."

"Oh, I wanted to," I say.

"But." Iris's mouth snaps shut. She takes her hand from the table and laces her fingers roughly, twisting them.

"Iris, *what is it?*" I say, feeling afraid with the sense of unknowing.

"Maybe you don't want this," she says.

"Tell me," I say.

She looks at me with an awful, desolate expression. And, though I don't know what's coming, I suddenly understand that Iris herself has been wearing some kind of uniform all the while I've known her. Perhaps she even forgot herself, if that's what she wanted — discarded herself in favor of something simpler. But somehow my Wrap-Up List has torn the veil. She's seen herself anew, and what's worse, she thinks this is the last moment of our friendship, because of what she's about to tell me. I suddenly flash back to that moment when I told her that I'd jump on a hand grenade for her. When she'd looked at me so seriously, and I'd looked away.

"That kiss," she says, her voice quivering. "It would have to be with a girl."

I open my mouth to respond before I've fully understood what she's just said. But when I do understand, no words emerge. Part of what leaves me speechless is that I never suspected it. In fact, I think I have never suspected this of anyone I've ever personally met. But as her words drop into me, I see the truth in a thousand recollections — her getting asked to freshman prom by so many guys and saying no to them all. Always finding fault with everyone who has a crush on her. I remember also the way she's always contriving small talk with Wendy. *Wendy.*

The other part of what leaves me speechless, though, is more shameful. I feel uncomfortable. I haven't ever known anyone like this. I think I didn't really believe in it. And *Iris,* of all people. She's so . . . so well-disguised.

"I . . . er . . ." says my jaw, abandoned by my brain.

"It's okay," says Iris. She returns to the card catalog and pulls a card out of it. "It doesn't matter." She says this with a heavy blankness, and I sense her retreating back inside herself.

Gabriela, I think, *you have got to do better than this.* I rally against the confounding invasion of surprise and shock. I reach out and again take Iris by the arm.

"It does matter," I say. I'm not thinking about what *it* is right now — I'm thinking only about my friend, her eyes red, standing miserably before me.

We stand frozen together, me with one hand on her arm, she looking down at my brown fingers on her pale skin. The room is silent. She's waiting to see if I reject her. And who knows if I could have? For a moment, I think I nearly did.

Now it's my turn to lunge clumsily forward. I throw my arms around her. *"I'm sorry!"* I blubber, apologizing for I'm not sure what — for something that almost happened.

We're both crying. And Iris likes girls. That fact has not yet begun to unfold. I feel it there, lodged deep, like a hard seed that doesn't yet know it's been planted.

"Why didn't you tell me before?" I say over her shoulder.

"I just . . ." says Iris, sniffling. "The stakes were high."

"Was it because I'm Catholic?" As I say the words, I think of my dad. He would not be pleased if he ever learned of this.

"Maybe," says Iris.

There's much more, but we've said enough for now. We fall silent, and step apart from each other, momentarily shy. Then Iris holds up the card she previously removed from the catalog. "I'm going to go get this," she says. She disappears into the shelves and a few moments later emerges holding an old manila file. *"Here,"* she says cheerfully. She lays it on the table and opens it.

It contains a single sheet of paper. "Hercule's last documented departure," she says. "This is a copy, not the original." She runs a red fingernail along the small lines of type.

Stops. Stares.

"Oh," she says.

"What?" I ask. She turns the page so I can see.

TRANSCRIPTION FROM OFFICIAL DOCUMENTS
PROVIDED BY: TUNISIAN DEPARTURE AUTHORITY
Attending Death: Hercule

Site: Tunisian Fields (Formerly Berber Fields of
Carthage), Olive Grove
Departing Person: Gonzalo Rivera. Citizenship:
   Mexico, residing USA
Departure Status: Pardoned. Trns. to————

"Gonzalo Rivera?" I say. "But . . . ?" I look at Iris.
"But . . . ?"

"I've never seen anything like this," she says, nervousness
in her voice.

"Hercule couldn't have been . . ."

"He was your grandfather's attending Death," she says
quietly.

"But Gonzalo didn't depart," I say. "He was killed in action."

"You never knew that for sure."

"Isn't there a thing about Deaths never visiting the same
family twice?"

"Yes, there is a thing," said Iris. "Deaths usually steer clear
of friends and relatives because they're worried people will find
out their Noble Weakness and share the information." Then
she points silently to the line that reads "Departure Status."

"Pardoned," I say. "But that doesn't make sense either. If he
was Pardoned, why didn't he come home?"

"The Pardon was transferred — that's what this means."
She points to the words "Trns. to."

"Transferred?"

"Your grandfather gave it away."

"You can do that?" I say. "But . . . who got it? It's blank."

"The Tunisian authority never found out. It was during the war, so it's lucky this record exists at all. Even luckier that a copy got sent here."

"I can't believe my dad never found this," I say.

"He wouldn't have known unless he was looking for something about Hercule," says Iris. "None of these are cross-referenced. But Gabriela, the main thing is that there was a Pardon issued. And that means—"

"My grandfather discovered Hercule's Noble Weakness."

I hear footsteps in the hall, and my dad rounds the corner. "I had a minute free, so . . ." He squints at us in the low yellow light. He can tell something's up.

I take the folder from Iris and hold it out to him.

four days before
departure day

meet me at the canal

The discovery that Gonzalo departed with Hercule is hugely important for my family. Dad makes a photocopy of the record. He shows Mom as soon as she gets home, and then he goes to Aunt Ana's to tell her and her family. When he returns from that, his eyes are red from crying. Grandfather Gonzalo's disappearance has been a loose thread in our lives for as long as I can remember. Now that thread has been pulled, and the mystery is more convoluted than ever. Pardoned—how? Pardon transferred—to whom? What happened to Gonzalo out there in the Tunisian Fields when he took his final walk with Hercule?

Needless to say, I have trouble getting to sleep. In my room in the wee hours, I spend some time staring at Hercule's Hints, and some time staring at my picture of Gonzalo. I put my head down on my desk and close my eyes. I think about Iris.

Her confession has me ruminating over our friendship, wondering about things that have happened between us. Times we've slept in the same bed together. Times Iris has called me cute. A weird, panicked feeling grows. I do not want to be . . . but if I am . . . (but I don't think so) . . . ? And the Church, it goes without saying. Years of Bible study. Dad. I remember one time when he and I were out walking—we saw two men holding hands. He muttered, under his breath, a word I hadn't heard before: *maricas*. I didn't know it, but his tone was one I never forgot: disgust.

Iris said, "Maybe you don't want this." And at the moment, tossing in bed and worried—not just about her but about myself, about my own nature—I understand something that she knew better than I. In telling me, she gave me something. I don't know what it is yet. It's only just starting to grow.

I'm not sure when I doze off, but I awaken with a start, jerking my head from my desk and blurting, *"Wha*z*at?"*

Morning sun streams through the windows. Its warmth on my back is what awakened me. I glance at my watch. Ten o'clock. I have a feeling there's . . . somewhere I'm supposed to be?

Then I remember: "meet me at the 45th street canal."

I don't have much time. I rush to the bathroom and look at the tired girl in the mirror, slumping under a mop of mussed hair. I attack my curls with a brush for a few minutes, reducing but not eliminating the thicket. I apply eyeliner and mascara, then pull on my favorite jeans and a long-sleeved shirt with fleur-de-lis designs stitched into it. I hope it's cute.

As I prepare, I wonder if maybe I needn't worry — with Hercule's Influence, I could probably show up wearing a barrel and a chicken mask and still look good. But my vanity won't allow this.

Mom and Dad are on the couch watching the weekend news report. "Morning," I say, a little awkwardly.

"Good morning, sweetie," says Mom. She and Dad both stand and hug me, which isn't what usually happens when I enter a room. "How are you feeling?" Mom asks.

"I don't know," I say. "Late, I guess."

"Late?"

"I'm meeting . . . Sarena. For coffee."

"Oh," says Mom, and I get the sense from her tone that she and Dad have been waiting around in hopes of having a talk with me.

"I'll be back," I say. "Back for dinner." Then I remember that I still haven't shown them Hercule's Hints. Maybe this is a good moment — just get it over with. But before I can enact this idea, Dad says, "I want to talk to you about Confession, Gabby. I'd like you to go before Mass tomorrow."

This startles me. Then it makes sense. Then it makes me mad, the presumptuousness of it. "I'll think about it," I say.

"This could be your last Confession, Gabriela," he says firmly. "You have to go. That's *final*." He's not joking. His eyes glow with frustration and fear.

"It won't be my last," I say, equally firm. "I'm going to confess plenty of things, for the rest of my life!" When I say *life*, my voice cracks. Seeing Dad's emotion has started me down the same path. I turn and stride quickly to the front door.

"Gabriela—" says Mom.

I'm gone.

The Snake River winds down wooded hillsides from Snake Lake, which lies near the mountain pass. When the river reaches town, it flows into a straight cement canal, which chaperones it through three neighborhoods and releases it to the southeast. The mile or so of its urban passage, known as "the canal," features gravel paths and a few overpasses. It's a popular place to go for a stroll, or for a talk.

Sylvester's right where he said he'd be. He's sitting on a metal bench wearing a green hooded sweatshirt and jeans. A burned-out cigarette dangles forgotten from his fingers. He's watching the stream of passing joggers, moms, and retirees that daily occupy the walking path. When I see him, I can scarcely believe he's here to meet *me*. He's the kind of person I always encounter by accident, whose orbit is unknowable. I stand at a distance for a while, watching him, convincing myself that I'm really supposed to walk up to him and say "Hi." I

give my hair a quick fluff and smooth my eyebrows. I walk up
to him.

"Hi," I say.

He absentmindedly ashes his extinguished cigarette. "Hi,"
he replies. He scoots over, inviting me to sit, which I do, my
skin prickling as I approach closer to him than I've ever been.
He smells of smoke, sweat, and soap, having come here straight
from football practice.

"So," he says, "which Death contacted you?"

"He's named Hercule," I reply. I sit patiently, hoping perhaps for some condolences, but Sylvester offers none. He puts
his cigarette to his lips and finally discovers that it's out. He
tosses it on the gravel and produces a pack from his shirt pocket. "Want one?" he asks.

"Sure." I've never smoked, but why not? Sylvester lights
one and passes it to me. I puff on it.

"Don't puff," he says. "Inhale."

Taking this advice starts me into a coughing fit. Sylvester
laughs as I hand the cigarette back. He holds it to his lips. Air
tumbles past the ember. When he exhales, he tells me why he's
asked me here. The explanation emerges with the smoke.

"I'm going to depart, too," he says. He sighs out the rest of
the breath. "I haven't told anyone."

I'm dumbfounded. Like my parents a few days back, I first
think that there's a mistake. My second thought is that Iris was
right—*finally right!*—about one of her suspicions.

"Which Death?" I say, not because it's an important question; it's just the first to jump into my head.

"Hercule," Sylvester replies.

"That . . . can't be," I say. Some totally obscure Death contacts both of us at once? But Sylvester does not appear to be putting me on. "That's my Death," I insist. "Not even Iris has heard of him."

"Yeah," says Sylvester, strangely unsurprised. "I tried to do some research, but forget it. It doesn't matter."

There are a million things I could say here, all foolish. As the catalog flits past my mind's eye, I select the most foolish of all and speak it before I have time to think twice. "Sylvester . . . I have . . . a . . . crush? On . . . um . . . *you.*"

His eyes widen. For a moment, he seems to be weighing whether or not this is a joke. Then, he smiles. "Well!" he proclaims. He sits up straight, and smoothes the front of his sweatshirt comically. He starts puffing his cigarette, clowning on the way I did it before (*puffpuffpuff*). "Why didn't you say anything?" he asks. (*Puffpuffpuff.*)

"I don't know," I say. "Shy, I guess."

He nods. "No time for that now," he says. He takes a long draw on the cigarette, and emits the smoke in a gray stream. "I have a question for you, Gabriela." He reaches into his pocket and produces a folded piece of paper. I recognize it instantly as he opens it. It's his Wrap-Up List, with Hercule's Hints scrawled on it. Sylvester's list contains many more items than mine. His first, at the very top, says, "Enlist in the Army." Hercule's Hint below that:

— *Volunteer.*

I recall Sylvester's question of Sergeant Mistletoe yesterday—whether there was any way to volunteer before turning eighteen. This is not the item to which Sylvester directs my attention now, though. He points at the bottom of the page, to the last line, which reads, as mine does, "Pardon." Below it, Hercule has scrawled the following Hint:

— *Wait for Gabriela.*

We observe this together.

"So I waited," says Sylvester, "and here you are."

"I . . . I . . ." I stutter. "Maybe some other Gabriela?" This seems highly unlikely. "I'm . . . I'm . . ." I'm not getting anywhere, but Sylvester helps me out:

" . . . hoping to get kissed?" he says. He squints at me, some of the humor returning to his eyes. "Is that on your Wrap-Up List, maybe?" He says this with a droll tone that I have difficulty interpreting—is he making fun? Showing off his deductive skills?

He stands, tosses his cigarette to the gravel, and stamps it out. "Have you been to the Fields?" he asks. He's not wondering if I've *ever* been there. He's wondering if I've been since I learned I was going to depart. I recall instantly the second half of Hercule's Hint about my first kiss: — *The Fields*.

"I'll drive," he says.

the fields

Sylvester opens the passenger door to his shiny red sports car for me, and I step in. The interior smells of new leather — an intoxicating, slightly nauseating scent.

I pull the seat belt across my lap as Sylvester starts the engine. He grins. "Safety first," he says as I click the strap into place. "You're marked for departure, you know."

"Better that than dying in a car crash today," I reply. Then, something occurs to me. "This car!" I exclaim. "Hercule got you this?"

"The dealership was raffling it," says Sylvester. "Hercule told me to buy a ticket, and I won." He backs the car from the parking stall, then guns the engine and races to the end of the lot. I place both hands on the dashboard and Sylvester chuckles, obviously getting some satisfaction from scaring me. We pull into the street, and he darts around two slower cars and runs a yellow light.

In moments, we're out of downtown, racing along the winding road toward the Fields. My initial fears fade as Sylvester's competence as a driver impresses itself upon me and I give in to the thrill of the trip. We speed through a neighborhood of warehouses and finally curve into the pinewoods and onto a bumpy, single-lane road.

The sun diminishes in a high mist, and its sharp light fades. It's almost always foggy out here. As we go deeper into the woods, colors fade to gray. Fog curls onto the road. Sylvester hits his headlights but doesn't slow. Branches scrape the sides of the car. The fuzzy lights of an oncoming sedan appear, and it blips by, driven by a woman about my mom's age. Her red taillights shrink away behind us.

Soon, we reach the parking lot. Sylvester decelerates across the gravel and parks, and we step out into the cold. It's drizzling here, and the drops of rain pop against the roof and the ground. Sylvester stands next to me. "Come on," he says. He offers me his arm, and I take it.

Immediately beyond the parking lot is a gazebo set in a small rose garden, where class field trips usually start. We look at the map there, which shows the public Fields stretching out to a dotted line labeled DEPARTURE. Only Deaths and departing people can go beyond that, and no one returns from there. That is, no one beyond the very few who earned Pardons at the last moment and walked back. There's rumored to be a grove of oaks out there.

Sylvester and I wander among the roses, where a few bushes

try to bloom in the fog. "I hope it doesn't rain," I say. Sylvester is quiet, but I can tell he understands that I'm not referring to right now. "I just don't see *why*," I add. "Why *us*."

"I tried to ask Hercule when I wrote to him," says Sylvester, "but . . ." He trails off, indicating that Hercule's response was unsatisfactory. "It's not worth worrying about."

"Yeah." Everything I've ever read on this subject reaches a similarly inconclusive conclusion. Some people just get chosen. Young. Old. Rich. Poor. White. Brown. Americans. Russians. Mexicans serving in the U.S. Army deployed in Tunisia.

My hair is wet from the drizzle, and a damp chill penetrates my clothes. I shiver, and Sylvester puts an arm around me as we proceed onto the lawn. Anyone can come here, so the city maintains it, mowing and watering the turf. The grass is loaded with moisture, and after a few steps my feet are wet.

The rose garden disappears behind, and we're surrounded by the small circle of grass we can see through the fog. The ground grows rougher as we walk, and the even, green turf turns to a scrubby, shorn field. I don't see the sign until it's right in front of us: DEPARTURE. Beyond, the unshorn grass grows waist high, brown and dead from winter, out of range of the city's lawn mowers.

Stacked by the edge are countless piles of rocks — cairns built up by the relatives of departing souls.

I release Sylvester's arm and step to the dividing line. I push forward, and feel the invisible resistance of the boundary — it pushes back at you, like you're lying on the surface of a pool, too buoyant to sink. The deeper you press, the more firmly it presses back. No one knows how these forces work, though plenty of people study them.

I lean in and float there in the air. *Not yet, Gabriela,* the boundary seems to say, holding me off.

Sylvester joins me. He stretches out his arms as he leans in, too, letting the boundary support him. "My dad went to the Fields a few times in Vietnam," he says. "I guess they bring lotus flowers for the person, instead of stacking rocks."

"Was he in the war?" I ask.

"Yeah."

"You want to go, too," I say. "You asked about enlisting in class."

Sylvester shakes his head, and a lock of hair falls along the firm line of his nose. I resist a strong inclination to reach out and brush it aside, to touch his cheek. "He doesn't want me to, but I'm going to do it. I'll trick him into being proud of me."

"Trick him?"

"The old man," says Sylvester. He smiles humorlessly. "I doubt anyone else could understand. It's between us."

"Try me," I say.

Sylvester glances over, and I return his gaze. After my role as confidante to Iris yesterday, I'm feeling like I can handle almost anything.

"Well, it doesn't make sense," he says, "but just try to believe it makes sense to *me.*"

"Okay."

"My dad's angry—about his arm. He always has been. His missing arm, you know? *The Arm.* When I was a kid, he told me it was the military's fault he lost it. That they could have saved it if there'd been a decent medic in the field. He blames his arm for all kinds of stuff—Mom leaving him, losing his job. So, there's that." Sylvester pauses, then continues. "The other thing is, he blames *me* for stuff, too. Sometimes the same stuff. I know it sounds crazy, but I think I *am* that arm. Like his own fingers. But I never do things right." Sylvester's voice descends as he says this, and his eyes narrow. "But I'll show him. I'm going to enlist. And I'm going to be a *medic*." He looks over at me, to check my response to this. "*The Arm* is going back out there. It's going to do what he wishes it had done."

I think my face is blank. Sylvester's right—it doesn't make sense . . . but it does, in a way. It reminds me of something I learned in catechetics class, and I quote it aloud now from memory: "If thine enemy hunger, feed him . . . : in so doing thou shalt heap coals of fire on his head."

Sylvester looks surprised. "What's that?" he says.

"St. Mary's," I say. "We memorized verses about service. I like that one, because you're being nice to be mean."

"Yeah, that's it," says Sylvester. "Not that it matters any-way—turns out I'm departing the day before I turn eighteen."

"When?"

"Tomorrow," he says, with pronounced casualness. "Tomorrow at midnight. During the fight."

"During the fight?" I repeat, emphasizing each word. I don't know why it surprises me, but it does. *The fight!* It's a forbidden event, after the last game of the season. I didn't go last year, but I heard it whispered about. It happens at midnight, on the football field, between the Cougars football team and whoever they just played (this year, the South High Jaguars).

"Hercule's going to take me right off the field!"

"Have you told *anyone?*" I ask. "Your dad?"

"Yeah, I told him. I didn't want to, but I kind of had to." He pauses. "What about you? Have you talked to Hercule about *your* date?"

"Next Wednesday," I say.

"Ah," he says, closing his eyes to imagine how great it must be to have so much time.

We fall silent, neither sure what to say, bodies pressing into the boundary, floating in midair.

Then, I smell it. The blooms—the hyacinths, or hydrangeas, or whatever they are. The scent is really strong, and I wonder if they grow out *there*, out past the boundary, but my wonderment is overwhelmed by the effect of the scent upon me. I feel like I'm waking up after a long nap. My body fills with sensation.

I turn to face Sylvester, looking at him for the first time without reserve, drinking him up. He is achingly, unbelievably beautiful. I reach out and touch his shoulder as he, also, breathes deep. When I have his attention, I take a step back from the boundary and sit on the wet, brown grass. The cold damp immediately soaks through my jeans, but I scarcely notice.

He joins me, kneeling next to me.

"Do you smell the blooms?" I ask.

His clear eyes are locked onto me. I'm close enough to see small beads of water poised at the ends of his eyelashes.

He leans toward me. His breath smells of cigarettes—not a stale smell but a rich one, mixing with the sweat and soap of football practice, and now with the stinging profusion of the unseen blossoms. As he draws near, I close my eyes . . .

Suddenly he grabs my shoulders. My eyes snap open to see him grinning before me, prankish. I pull back. "Hey!" I say.

"Is this going to be your *very first kiss?*" he says, leering comically.

I twist in his grasp, confused. "Quit it," I say.

Before he can respond, we're interrupted.

A foot bumps into my shoulder, and from above there's a surprised exclamation. Someone is falling over us, wheeling around and landing hard. Sylvester and I quickly uncompromise ourselves, wide-eyed, to see a tall, slim figure on the ground.

It is a Death.

"*Of all the*—" he curses, wallowing in the wet grass.

"I'm *sorry!*" I say, as the creature collects himself. He stands, smoothing his gray suit, glaring. He extends a scornful silver finger toward us, frowning, eyes smoldering, before stalking off into the fog in the direction of the parking lot, still straightening his pants.

Sylvester and I sit as silent as stones, startled nearly out of our skins. Then he makes a sudden hissing sound, like air coming out of a bicycle tire. He's . . . laughing! His eyes bug. He wheezes.

It hadn't occurred to me that this was funny, but when it does, I let out a sudden snort. We quickly become hysterical. Our voices boom into the fog. It feels good. I'm sure the Death hears us as he makes his morbid way toward town.

"His *expression!*" I croak.

"He was *pissed!*" Sylvester gasps.

It's a long time before we've recovered. I think it must be the funniest thing that's ever happened.

could have beens

I'm home for dinner, as promised. It's a quiet affair at first, Mom, Dad, and I focused on our plates, which contain fettuccine with Alfredo sauce. Mom doesn't usually cook, but sometimes, if Dad comes home late from work, she'll rise to the occasion and make fettuccine with Alfredo sauce. I twirl my fork among the milky strands.

"I'll go to Confession tomorrow," I say.

Confession has never been my favorite sacrament (or even my seventh favorite). But it will ease Dad's mind, I know. And although I'm expecting to get a Pardon, as the days pass I . . . I want to wrap things up right, just in case.

"Thank you, Gabriela," says Dad, to his pasta. "That means a lot to me. It's the right thing."

"Dad," I say, "have you thought any more about Gonzalo? What Iris and I found?"

"Ana called today to talk more," he says. "We can't believe it. After all these years."

"You never suspected his death was a departure."

"No, never."

"Or that he was Pardoned."

"By *Hercule,*" Mom jumps in.

There's a pause. Mom and Dad are both looking at me. Again, I realize I haven't shown them my Wrap-Up List, or Hercule's Hints. But I'm going to now. It's time.

Without saying anything, I stand and fetch the list and Hints from my room. I hand it to Mom, and Dad leans over her shoulder. They read it. And they think . . . Oh, I don't know what they think. I can't stand it. "So, there you go!" I say.

"Have you and Iris gotten any ideas about your Pardon?" says Dad.

"Not yet," I say.

We fall silent. Mom passes the page back to me. This is awful. I can't believe I thought my list was such a great idea before.

"Gabriela, are you still planning to go to the football game tomorrow night?" Mom asks.

"I think so," I say.

"Your father and I have decided *not* to go," she says. "We talked it over. We want you to enjoy it with your friends."

"Oh, that's not—" I say. I can tell that "We talked it over" really means "We argued about it."

"That's final," says Dad. He smiles sadly.

I want to protest further, but I don't. It will make things easier if they aren't there. "I might spend the night at Iris's house afterwards," I say, crafting a quick alibi against attending the midnight fight. Then I revise, "Actually, at *Sarena's* house." I don't know at first what prompts this revision, but as soon as I realize, I feel awful. I'm so at loose ends about Iris that I'm avoiding even an imaginary overnight with her. I am a rotten person. "Actually," I re-revise, "it *is* at Iris's house, I just remembered, but, um, we're starting at Sarena's house? Then going to Iris's house after that?"

My parents watch as I flounder before them for no apparent reason.

Just before bed, the phone rings. Dad answers, and holds it out to me. "It's Iris," he says.

I put the receiver to my ear. "Hi," I say.

"Hi."

"Um, how are you?" I ask, feeling awkward.

"I've been thinking about your grandfather," says Iris, jumping right in with high enthusiasm. "It's like nothing I've ever heard of! And get this — I did some more research into Hercule's other departures."

"You did?" I say. It hadn't even occurred to me to do more research.

"In the last three hundred years, he's given two Pardons aside from your grandfather's. And *both were also transferred.*"

"You mean, both were given away?" I say.

"Right. It might not mean anything, but it's quite a coincidence, don't you think?"

"Ugh," I say, reeling from what seems an endless parade of unknowables. "I wish we could somehow . . . I don't know, *kidnap* him. Tie him up and . . . and force him to tell us!"

Iris laughs musically. "That would be great," she says. Then there's a long pause. "Wait just a *second.*"

I wait. "Iris? Are you still there?"

"Gabriela," she says, her voice a whisper. "What if we really could?"

"Could what?" I say.

"Kidnap him."

"What are you talking about?" I'm whispering now, too.

"I need to think about this more . . . but just tell me — *would* you?"

"I . . . Yes, I would," I say.

"Meet me tomorrow. At Marking Street, after you're done with church."

Click — the line goes dead without even a goodbye.

"Gabriela?" says Dad from the kitchen. "Everything all right?"

Funny question.

Mom, Dad and I end up in the living room later, watching TV. The news reports are distressing, and it's unavoidable that we start talking about the war. But Mom and Dad don't agree — they never do.

"Yes, dear," says Dad to Mom, "but what you don't understand is that war can save lives."

"Maybe it can, but it never does," says Mom.

"No one can know the future," says Dad.

"So there you are," says Mom.

"I'm going to bed," I say, standing.

I brush my teeth and change into my pajamas, feeling the emotional coldness blowing in from the otherwise silent living room, where the TV blithely continues. Mom and Dad are making a show of reading magazines, but they aren't really reading. They're thinking about what they could have said to win the argument.

I think my parents have an okay relationship overall, but sometimes I wonder — they went through so much to be together, with Dad enduring the racism of Mom's parents, and Mom converting to Catholicism. Seeing them bicker over the evening news is sad. As the years pass, the marriage they fought for is settling into acid.

It makes me think again about uniforms. When Mom and Dad fell in love, was it with the person or with some disguise put on to impress? On the other hand, maybe they really did love each other, and now they've forgotten — each presumptively dressing the other in the uniform of their own annoyance. When do you see the person, and when the façade? I'm not sure if I know what those terms mean anymore.

I return to my room and sit on the edge of my bed. I take

out my rosary, but I don't pray. Instead, I remember something from last year—another time when Ms. Lime and I were meeting to talk about my difficult transition into high school. My parents were arguing more than ever, and I think my own troubles were the cause of some of it. They were both worried about me. I really don't think Mom and Dad would ever get divorced, but things were bad back then, and that subject was on my mind. It just seemed like they'd get tired of arguing and call it quits. I was seething about this when I met with Ms. Lime. I could barely speak, just stared vengefully out the window. Ms. Lime said, "Gabriela, sometimes regular words aren't enough. Sometimes when I'm really upset, I write poetry. Do you ever write poetry?"

This struck me as a stupid idea, and in a snit I snatched up a pencil from Ms. Lime's desk and scribbled a little haiku on a pink sticky note (five syllables, seven, five). I still remember it:

> *Divorce divorce div*
> *orce divorce divorce divorce*
> *Divorce divorce div*

I shoved it across the table. Ms. Lime read it. After a moment, she said, "You're right, Gabriela. Divorce doesn't fit."

I've been interested in writing ever since.

· · ·

When the memory finishes, I return my rosary to my desk, close my bedroom door, turn out the light, and slip under the covers.

I'm wide awake. There's too much swirling in my head, and each thought sends me onto a different tangent, but the strongest is this: I thought I was going to get kissed today. Everything added up—both of Hercule's Hints seemed fulfilled—and then Sylvester was a jerk. Why did he grab me like that? Why make a joke about it? It doesn't make sense. It's cruel.

I remember the way he held out his arm so chivalrously in the parking lot. There was something awkward about that, as if he were imitating a movie . . .

Finally, I get it. Maybe I didn't see it before because it didn't seem possible, since Sylvester is a senior. But as Sherlock Holmes said, when you've eliminated the impossible, whatever remains, however improbable, must be the truth. And the truth is: Sylvester was *nervous*, because he likes me.

I envision us again walking into the fog of the Fields, to the boundary. The smell of flowers blows from the unknown glade. We sit together in the cold. Jewels of water cling to his pretty eyelashes.

I imagine what I wish had happened. That it had been tender. That Sylvester was confident and gentle. That he leaned in slowly. That his soft lips touched mine.

three days before
departure day

confession

Mom, Dad, and I are up early. They dress in their nice church clothes, whereas I wear a warm outfit appropriate for the football game later on (jeans, long-sleeved shirt, sweater, parka). We ride the old elevator to the lobby, step onto the staircase at the front of the building, and stop. We stare down into the street.

Usually the neighborhood is empty when we leave for early Mass, but today things prove a far cry from the usual. Instead of the peaceful, quiet lull of a day yet to begin, there are hundreds, maybe thousands, of people walking by, filling both traffic lanes and both sidewalks. They're all dressed in black. It's a human river, confusing and beautiful for a moment until I see the signs and banners, and the surreality dissipates. I glance at Dad in time to see him draw the same conclusion as I: this is a protest march, against the war.

"We'll have to walk with them for a couple blocks," says

Dad. The *we* and *them* of his statement clearly express not only his sympathies but mine and Mom's by extension. Not even a week ago I'd have felt perfect solidarity with him on this point. Dad sees what I used to see — the nobility. Maybe he has to believe in that, for the sake of his own father. But more and more I'm seeing something different.

We descend the front steps and join the march. We do not match the uniform of the occasion, as Dad is dressed in brown, Mom in green, and I in blue.

Immediately ahead of us, carried over the crowd by a group of pallbearers, is a long black coffin. We skirt around it. Stenciled across the side are the words SONS AND DAUGHTERS.

As we go by, I notice something about one of the pallbearers. He's marching precisely on the left side of the coffin. One sleeve of his black jacket is pinned up, empty. It's Mr. Hale, Sylvester's dad. His face is tired, his chin dusted with stubble. I wonder if Sylvester knows his father is out here protesting the war he wants to volunteer for.

Soon Mom, Dad, and I turn off the route of the march, toward St. Mary's. There's another group standing at the intersection, with signs that indicate their opposition to the marchers, and their support of the war. They seem less organized, not all dressed any particular color or trying to create a spectacle beyond their hasty-looking placards. As we pass, my dad nods to one of them, a man wearing a fly-fishing vest with a sign that says SOME THINGS ARE WORTH FIGHTING FOR.

• • •

The humble bulk of St. Mary's looms before us minutes later, and we enter.

Our parish is a mix of middle- and low-income people, including a significant population of Mexicans and Koreans. I've noticed that ethnicity influences people's seating choices. Our church, like lots of Catholic churches, is called cruciform, which means it's cross shaped, with the altar in the middle (at the intersection of the metaphorical crossbeams). The short arms of the cross, areas called transepts, each contain rows of seats. I was still a kid when I noticed that we always sat with Aunt Ana and her husband, Hector, in the west transept, with other Latino families. The east transept, across the way, is where the Koreans sit, and the long middle, the seating down what's called the nave, is everybody else—mostly white people of Irish and English descent.

These divisions are partly linguistic. If you look at the missals everyone follows the service with, there are Spanish translations in the west transept, Korean ones in the east transept, and English in the nave. One thing I kind of like about the early service at St. Mary's is that the Mass is performed in Latin. It doesn't matter what language you speak — God is from Rome.

Plenty of parishioners are turned out for early Mass today, and as is usually the case, it's an older crowd. I don't see many kids here. Most families seem to prefer the nine thirty or eleven o'clock service, both of which are in English. The early service is a little more like how things used to be, in the Church of antiquity: Latin, candles, and incense as compared to English, electricity, and incense. Incense is the common denominator. The strong, weighty frankincense burns into the air even now. It's interesting: to smell frankincense, and to experience the churchly state of mind it imparts, you have to come here. You choose it. You send yourself through these doors, where the wheezy organ blows. But the other smell I've been encountering lately — the flowers — that smell is ready to hijack you anywhere. It's blowing around in the wind, the organs of hydrangeas piping universally.

We dip our fingers in the font of holy water and genuflect before the altar. We find seats next to Ana, Hector, and their kids, Juan (eight years old) and Pia (thirteen months old). Ana and Hector are both friendly, plump people, and they both give me hugs — it's the first they've seen me since I got my Death Letter. My aunt's eyes look teary as she contemplates me.

Mom and Dad stand apart. I wonder what it's like to wake up in bed next to someone and know they're mad at you. Even as they regain consciousness after a solid night of slumber, their anger is waiting for them, like the morning paper full of what happened yesterday.

Dad glances at me and gestures significantly behind us to a door at the rear of the transept — the confessional.

Confession at St. Mary's is not like Confession in the movies. When I attended confirmation classes, we learned about the Second Vatican Council, which happened in the 1960s. It was a meeting where the Church decided to liberalize itself. Catholic rituals in movies are usually pre–Vatican II, when

Confession involved a closet with an opaque grating between you and the priest. At St. Mary's, Confession takes place in an office, where you meet with Father Ernesto or Father Salerno and talk things over.

Our family's priest has always been Father Ernesto. He pretty much *is* the Church for us Riveras, since forever. Sometimes though, I'll admit, Father Salerno is easier to deal with in Confession, partly because I don't know him very well, and partly because he doesn't speak Spanish.

I'm embarrassed that I don't have any Spanish beyond one semester of it last year in school. Neither Dad nor Aunt Ana ever encouraged me, though they're both fluent. It bothers me more and more. Six months ago, at the tail end of my largely miserable freshman year, my fifteenth birthday was coming up. Mom, Dad, and I were in the community hall after Mass, and this kid, Herman, about two years younger than me, asked me, "Gabriela, will you have your quinceañera here in the community hall?"

"Quinceañera?" I replied. "What's that?"

Herman looked at me like I was from Mars—but I didn't know what he was talking about. No one ever asked if I wanted a quinceañera any more than they'd asked if I wanted to be confirmed the year before that. I was simply not consulted about such things.

There's one person lined up in advance of me for Confession—a middle-aged white lady who's wearing knee-length boots and a purple dress. She enters the office and closes the door. Her confession lasts about ten minutes, and when she emerges our eyes meet briefly. We both think, *I'm curious about your sins.*

I take a deep breath of sanctifying frankincense and enter. The sounds of pre-Mass socializing are blocked as I close the door to find Father Ernesto sitting, waiting, an empty chair next to him.

Father Ernesto is like a force of nature. He knew Gonzalo. He was with Abuela when she passed away. He is, in his realm of authority, unquestionable. Today, he's wearing the robes of his office (white, with a colorful stole) over his black suit and priest's collar. He stands and hugs me. "Hola, Gabriela," he says. "It's good to see you." He gestures to the empty chair. He probably arranges this carefully — facing him, but not facing him too much. Given the gravity of all he hears, I'm sure he's had plenty of practice selecting an angle that allows for hesitation but encourages disclosure. I sit in the chair to find it warm — the body heat of the woman who confessed before me is still radiating from it.

"How are you doing?" he asks, his voice friendly and concerned.

"All right," I say. "I'm still trying to figure out my Pardon."

"I hope it's God's will," says Father Ernesto. "Have you thought about receiving Extreme Unction, Gabriela?"

"Oh, I don't know about that . . ." I say.

"It's not just for old people, you know," Father replies, then pauses. "But this is not why you're here today," he says. He holds out one old hand, passing the conversation to me.

"I've missed Mass a few times," I confess. It's true that missing services is a sin, and I've used nonattendance as a smoke screen before, but it won't work today. Father Ernesto sits, waiting. It is time for me to decide what this is going to be about. I consider for a moment and finally say, "Father, I have a question. About what the Church believes. I have a friend——"

Father interrupts me, saying, "Is it really a friend, Gabriela, or is it you? Remember, the sanctity and privacy of Confession protects you."

"Oh, no," I say, polishing the air before me with both hands, "it really is a friend. *Not* me." Did I rush too quickly to say that? Would it be so bad for him to think it was me? I don't know. "I was wondering about the Church's stance. About people who . . . who prefer their same gender."

"I assume you mean this in an intimate sense," says Father Ernesto. "Is your friend a boy or a girl?"

The question surprises me. "Um, girl," I say. "That doesn't matter, though, does it?"

"No," says Father Ernesto, "but it is different for women sometimes. For a man, it absolutely cannot be——obviously it's a mortal sin. But for a woman, perhaps it's not always so serious."

I stare at him. I'd expected him to tell me that Iris's soul was

in jeopardy, but instead he seems to be saying . . . actually, I
don't know what he's saying. Is he saying women's sins count
for less? And that's a good thing? Questions vie with one another in my mind until I finally say, "I don't understand."

"Understanding is not always ours to enjoy," says Father
Ernesto. His tone gives me pause. It's a little harsh, clipped. He
sounds like Dad does with his "That's final" — getting mad
because he doesn't really know the answer.

When Iris told me about herself, it was like she'd planted
a seed of thought in me. And that seed has been resting ever
since. Now, in an instant, it opens.

Suddenly I *see* Father Ernesto. Maybe for the first time in
my life, I really see him. And he is not Father Ernesto. He is
Jaime Ernesto, wearing a priest's collar. He is a man, an old
man. He's giving me advice, and I am deciding . . . that he's
wrong.

"Thank you, Father," I say. "That's all I wanted to know."

Father Ernesto relaxes, thinking his battle won. "Thank
you for your confession, Gabriela," he says, though I've
scarcely confessed anything. He raises a hand and makes the
sign of the cross before me. "As God's instrument, and with
the power of the Holy Spirit, I pronounce your sins forgiven."
He pauses. "Let me say, Gabriela," he adds, "that we're each
given different struggles in life. One man struggles with one
thing, and another with another. As we live, we ask the Lord's
help."

I stand to leave, but pause. This may be the last conversation the two of us ever have, and there's something I need him to know. "Thank you for your advice all these years, Father. And for being so kind to my family."

"Of course, Gabriela."

"I'm growing up now," I continue. "I think, in the future, we might disagree about some things."

Father Ernesto smiles. "I suppose so," he says. I can see in his eyes that he understands what has just happened here.

the planning meeting

After church, I walk to the Marking Street Café, where I find Iris sitting by the window drinking tea. The sudden perspective that descended upon me in the confessional is still with me. I feel like I'm seeing her for the first time. My best friend.

As I sit, Iris reaches into her shoulder bag and produces a few magazines, with plain covers but for their title: *The Journal of the Association of Departure Science*. Iris is the only person I know who quarterly wades through this publication, reading articles such as "Interchange Superalterability: An Exclusion-Based Analysis" and "The Infinite Field Hypothesis, viz. Atemporality."

"Iris," I say, "before we get into that, there's something I need to ask you. Something . . . sort of personal."

Iris lifts her cup and blows on the tea. "Go ahead," she says.

"When you said, um . . . when you said it would have to be a girl. I was wondering, well . . . I was wondering what you think of *Wendy.*"

Iris's cup becomes very heavy, and it pulls her arm to the table. She smiles, and really doesn't need to say anything more. She gestures toward the magazines she's brought. "Let's talk about what I mentioned on the phone," she says.

"Kidnapping . . . ?" I say.

"I think we can do it," she says. "I'm putting some ideas together, from different places. I don't know if anyone's ever tried it, but I think if we give Hercule the right . . . *encouragement,* we could drag him into our world a little early."

"Encouragement?" I say.

"First, I'll get together a list of all of Hercule's known departures. And we should perform the summoning in your venue — the place you're going to depart from."

"But I don't know where that is," I say.

"Where do you *want* to depart from? Usually people get to choose."

This gives me a shiver, as I recall Sylvester's upcoming departure from the football field, scheduled to transpire in just a handful of hours. I almost tell Iris about it, but I stop myself, feeling bound to respect his desire for secrecy. "Hey," I say, as I realize something.

"What is it?" says Iris.

"The first letter I got from Hercule. Do you remember?

The last sentence — we thought he was joking. *Save a dance for me*. I think he was being serious. I think . . . I think I'm going to depart from the Caballero."

Iris's face lights up. "It must be!" she says. She claps her hands together. "And we need to bring something Hercule has touched — your Death Letter, I think. Do you still have it? Oh my god, Gabriela — we are going to do this!"

"But how will we get into the Caballero? We can't just perform a summoning out on the dance floor — " I cut myself off, as, at that instant, the answer to my question enters the café.

Sarena is carrying her trumpet case, and has her band uniform slung over one arm. She waves to us as she lines up to get coffee. Iris and I watch her place her order. She brings her steaming cup to our table, where she consumes it in one businesslike gulp. Then she finally notices how intensely we're observing her.

"Hi, Sarena," says Iris.

"Hi, Sarena," I say.

She looks back and forth between us. "What is it?"

"Can I ask you for a favor?" I say.

the game

Iris, Sarena, and I walk to campus, brimming with
excitement over our plan to sneak into the Caballero tomorrow night and kidnap my Death. It's almost enough to make
me forget that within a few hours we're going to witness
Sylvester's departure.

The parking lot is starting to fill with cars already: kids in
the band, or on the team, who have to show up early, and a few
people who like to tailgate. I see a familiar hatchback. There's
Raahi with some friends, seniors I don't know very well, leaning against his back bumper. In his trunk are fixings for hamburgers and a jug of punch. Raahi holds up his glass toward us.

"Punch?" he says.

"We're headed to the music building," I say.

Raahi turns to his friends. "Watch my car," he says. He
quickly pours each of us a glass of punch, hands them around,
and walks with us.

"Raahi," I say, once we're out of earshot of the parking lot, "we're going to kidnap my Death tomorrow night, and I was wondering if—"

"*What?*" he says, punch sloshing from his cup.

"Oh, right," I say. I've gotten so used to the idea already, I forgot it might be unexpected. "Yeah—Iris and I figured out how. So, anyway, I was wondering if—"

"*Kidnap* your *Death?*" says Raahi. We've stepped under a breezeway that connects the main campus to the music building, and Raahi lays a steadying hand on one of the metal supports. He looks from one of us to the next, searching for a clue that we're joking.

"*Right,*" I say firmly.

"So, can you give us a lift to the Caballero?" says Sarena. "Around two or three in the morning?"

"And then stick around to help out?" says Iris.

"Help . . . out?" says Raahi.

"Help tie him up, for instance, once we've got him," says Iris.

"You guys . . ." says Raahi. He shakes his head in disbelief. He drinks the remainder of his punch. "All right," he says. "Count me in."

We arrive at the music building shortly after, to see many members of the marching band congregating by the front doors. Sarena greets them.

"See you after halftime," I say.

She hugs me. "See you then."

Raahi accompanies Sarena to the doors of the music building. As I watch them go, something occurs to me.

"What are you looking at?" Iris asks.

"Them," I whisper, gesturing.

"What about . . ." says Iris, and then: "Oh . . . *really?*"

"I think so," I say. And it *is* so. I'm surprised I hadn't put it together before. Raahi has a crush on Sarena.

Our school is nuts for football. I know there are other sports, but does anyone play them? We like football so much that it was we Cougars who years ago spearheaded an extended season in our division, which starts in September and doesn't wind up until March. More kids get to play, more kids get to cheer, and more kids start to care about football. We've sent lots of students to college on football scholarships, and some Cougars have even played in the NFL.

Our athletics field was the most expensive project Central High ever undertook. It cost more than the school itself, actually. The field is built into the hill, with the home team seating dug in on the uphill side and the away team seating on bleachers on the downhill side. The field between is presently lit with blaring halogen lights a hundred feet overhead. It's perfectly even, perfectly mowed, and perfectly green. The lines of play are precisely limed.

Iris and I visit the concession stand, which has just opened.

There's already a line of dressed-up kids standing next to their dates (or hoping their dates are on the way, or hoping someone will ask them out).

We buy sodas, and while Iris stops by the bathroom, I climb about halfway up the home seats, to our regular spot next to the railing. Beyond the bleachers to my left stretches the scrubby, undeveloped hillside, already darkening as the sun drops. Straight ahead, across the perfect green rectangle of the football yardage, the visiting side is starting to fill with a colorful patchwork of parkas. I recognize some of the people over there from church — Latino faces hailing from the South End — and I hear snippets of Spanish.

I take my Wrap-Up List from my pocket and spend a few moments contemplating it. The most frustrating Hint at the moment is the one that seems to hold the most promise — Hercule's identical responses to all of my "first kiss" entries.

— *A cavalier request, Gabriela.*

As Spanish phrases continue to float my way from across the field, my long-slumbering language skills very unexpectedly begin to stir (*Yawn! Did someone say something? Wow, I've been asleep for a while — look how long my hair is!*).

Cavalier. I stare at the word on my Wrap-Up List. "*Caballero,*" I whisper.

"What'd you say?" Iris asks as she slides into the seat next to me.

I'm thrilled, and suddenly a little playful. I fold the list quickly and return it to my pocket with an ironic glance. "That's classified, miss," I say.

"Did you just figure something out?" says Iris. "Tell me!"

I smile silently.

Within twenty minutes the concession stand has a line thirty people deep, and the only vacancy in the home bleachers is a reserved block at the front, which the marching band now enters to occupy. The crowd cheers, and Iris and I stand and yell, "Sarena! Sarena!" when she appears. I see Wendy, too. Since she's both a musician and a cheerleader, she has special permission to wear her cheer outfit in the marching band. Her short sleeves and miniskirt are tough to miss.

Raahi joins us as Ms. Garibaldi, the band director, raises her baton.

"Were you hanging out with Sarena this whole time?" I ask.

"Yeah," he says casually.

The band members raise their instruments, and a voice booms over the field from the announcer's booth. "Ladies and gentlemen, please stand for the playing of the national anthem." Everyone, on both sides of the field, rises. I've been through this many times, and it has never occurred to me to wonder about it, but looking down on the field now, with its demarcations, and across at families I know from St. Mary's, as we all ritualistically cover our hearts . . . it's just like church.

When the first notes are played, everyone, and everything, comes to a halt. People walking toward their seats stop walking. The football players gathered by the sidelines stand still. The concession stand stops vending. Every hand covers every heart, and everyone in the whole place is thinking, *We are about to go to war.*

I don't know what to feel. There are young people here, like Raahi, who have received draft letters. There are probably people here who were in this morning's protest march, too. I glance at Raahi. His expression is unreadable.

Sarena nails the high note, and everyone, I'm sure, mentally places the word that belongs there: *free.* This field, divided into yards. All of us here to root for our teams. The new insight I was granted this morning is still with me, and as I look around now, I clearly see the nature of this strange spectacle. I remember, not even a week ago, thinking it was silly to argue over something as self-evident as *victory.* But now I see. The players, the cheerleaders, the band, even the crowd — this entire stadium and everything that takes place in it is a uniform we have all decided to put on together. To forget ourselves.

As the ritual of Mass prepares the congregation to receive the Body of Christ, so the cheer squad prepares the fans to receive the varsity team. The cheerleaders spring onto the empty field, vigorous in their blue uniforms, skirts, and white gloves, gathering at the fifty-yard line and leading the spectators on both sides in a round of "We've Got Spirit, How About You?"

Then the starting teams—our defense and the Jaguars' offense—take the field. Normally I feel great excitement at this point, an impatience for things to get started. But not tonight. As Sylvester jogs on, fans in the home bleachers stand and hoot, and my blood runs cold. It's awful to imagine what he must be feeling as he begins the last hours of his life.

The whistle blows, and the game begins.

The first quarter is a little boring. Sylvester doesn't do much. Each team scores a field goal, and Iris and I drink our sodas. Things remain tied up through the second quarter. During this stretch, I begin to hear sounds from the hillside to the left of the bleachers: voices, shouts, and laughter. I peer into the semidark and see a bunch of kids playing their own football game out there in the patchy overflow light. These are the little brothers and sisters of the players on the field. Many of them I recognize—some are siblings of kids from school, and some are from St. Mary's. They're all mixed together, boys and girls. I nudge Iris and direct her attention to this alternative spectacle.

"Hey!" she calls over to the kids. "What are your teams called?" This question, shouted from out of nowhere, proves confusing. The kids look at one another first, and then toward us, shielding their eyes against the field lights. I repeat Iris's question, louder: "What are your teams called?"

"No names," a little boy yells back, his brown face nearly obscured by the hood of his sweatshirt.

"These aren't real teams," explains the girl next to him, maybe his older sister.

The kids go into a huddle. The girl who shouted appears to be the quarterback of the team with the ball. She holds one hand flat like a football field and diagrams a strategy on her palm with her index finger. They make their play, tossing a blue plastic football along the hillside, retreating into the shadows. I watch until they disappear. I wonder how that girl will endure her transformation from player into cheerleader as she gets older—all of these kids gradually mapping themselves onto the spectacle that's being demonstrated for them on the real field.

The second quarter ends. Once the teams exit, the announcer says: "Now, under the direction of Nadine Garibaldi, your Cougars Marching Band!" Ms. Garibaldi stands at the front of the bleachers, and the band takes the field in rows. Sarena is right after the drum major, and we all stand and shout: "Sarena! Sarena!" Neighboring fans look over, amused by our enthusiasm.

The band moves through its formations, spelling Go! and Win! with their bodies (in both cases, Wendy, in her cheer uniform, is the dot on the exclamation point). They zip expertly through "Baby Elephant Walk" and other marching treacle. When they finish and make their exit, the cheerleaders replace them, initiating a spirited call and response on "Fight! Fight! Fight!" (fight, fight, fight).

Iris and I go for more soda and find Sarena in line at the concession stand. She's taken off her tall marching hat, but is otherwise still dressed in full regalia—brass buttons, epaulets, creases.

"Go!" I say, as we reach her.

"Win!" says Iris.

Being in the band must be weird. You're simultaneously respected and mocked for it. And Sarena is like that, too—a cool dork.

The three of us return to the stands, where Raahi congratulates Sarena on her performance and invites her to sit next to him, which she does.

The game resumes. Sylvester is subbed out, and I watch him on the sidelines, talking with teammates and joking around. He seems perfectly normal. At the end of the quarter, he approaches Coach Frank and asks to be sent back in.

The coach assents, and the final quarter commences with the Cougars in possession on the Jaguars' eighteen-yard line. The whistle blows. The ball is hiked. Sylvester runs long, sprinting straight to the end zone. The quarterback, Jeff Dounais, scrambles as a hole appears in the defensive line. Jaguars pour through. Jeff panics and launches the ball in an overpowered pass, above the heads of the players. The moment the pass is released and its poor trajectory becomes clear, the fans start thinking about the next play; this one is as good as over.

So it's a surprise when Sylvester jumps for it. And it gets even more surprising. His body sails into the air. His fingers stretch. They intersect with the ball, and pull it down. He lands hard, falls, rolls, and stands.

Touchdown!

The crowd, after a moment of startled disbelief, goes bonkers. I cheer, too, but my excitement is tempered by something no one else knows: Sylvester can't jump that high. I expect that catching an impossible game-winning touchdown pass was on his Wrap-Up List.

The game is more or less in the bag. After Sylvester's catch, the quality of play diminishes. The teams aren't thinking about this match anymore. They're thinking about what comes next: the fight, at midnight.

the fight

After a few last-minute time-outs, the final whistle blows. The crowd slips the bonds of spectatorship. Parents walk onto the field to say hi to the players. Children chase one another up and down the yards. The game from the hillside briefly and gloriously reinvents itself on the now-vacant field. The cash register rings for the last time, and the lights in the concession stand go out. Engines turn over in the distant parking lot.

Iris, Raahi, Sarena, and I climb off the bleachers and walk around behind, in the shadows, where some other kids are loitering. I see Wendy nearby, with a few cheerleaders. We don't really know one another very well, and she looks surprised when I approach.

"Gabriela," she says, "I was so sorry to hear about your departure."

"Oh, that," I say dismissively. "I'm going to get a Pardon. Listen, I wanted to invite you — I'm going to be at the Caballero on Wednesday. The Washington Fifteen are playing. If you want to come, and anyone else . . ."

"Definitely!" says Wendy. I can tell she's touched that I invited her. "I'll bring a bunch of people."

I turn my gaze toward the bright green field. It's continuing to empty quickly. There's barely anyone left. Parents are gone. School officials and the groundskeepers are disappearing fast. It's so strange — everyone knows what's going to happen, but no one does anything to stop it.

"Are you staying for the fight?" I ask.

"All the cheerleaders are," she says, a note in her voice that suggests she isn't thrilled about it.

When I return to my friends, they're curious — especially Iris. "What was that about?" she asks.

"I invited Wendy to my departure," I say. "And you guys, too, if you want to bring any guests or anything, I hope you will — to the Caballero."

"Really?" says Sarena, struck.

"I think it's a good place to do it," I say.

"Well, I'll bring a fifteen-piece jazz orchestra with me!" she says.

"Gabriela," says Raahi, "I want to be there, but . . ." He doesn't finish. He doesn't have to.

"Oh, Raahi!" I say. "God, I can't believe—I didn't think—"

"It's okay."

"You're leaving . . ."

"Tuesday morning," he says.

Then: *wham!* The field lights turn off. It's easy to forget that none of the game here could have happened except for these lights. A hazy crescent moon and the dots of a few stars now glow above, but all that remains of the world down here is black and purple shadows.

"Whoa," I say but am drowned out by the *whoa*s of everyone around me.

"Right on cue," says Sarena. "There's only us kids here, now. We can head out front."

"If we can find the front," says Iris.

"Never fear!" says Sarena, and she flicks on a flashlight. It must be fun to be in the band and know about these things in advance.

Everyone who was standing in the nearby shadows, maybe twenty kids, walks to the field, while other flashlights descend from campus. It's ghostly and beautiful to see them accumulate at the base of the home bleachers, at the fifty-yard line. It's so dark that I can barely see across the field.

"What happens now?" Iris asks.

"We wait," Sarena replies. "The teams are already in the end zones."

"I'm kind of dreading this," I say.

"Everyone is," says Sarena.

I imagine Jaguars and Cougars gathering nervously out there in the black.

The audience grows to about a hundred kids. Sarena stands, looking for her fellow musicians. There are about fifteen members of the marching band here, and they walk onto the field now with members of the cheer squad.

Everyone's uniforms are deliberately disheveled. Some cheerers have only one glove on, or one shoe. One girl has replaced her miniskirt with blue jeans, and has put the skirt around her neck like a collar. Band members have their coats on backwards, or half-draped off their shoulders. The sousaphone player has his pants around his ankles, boxer shorts extending from the bottom of his blue coat, bare legs pale.

The band begins the national anthem. It sounds terrible. The instruments are out of tune, and everyone is purposefully playing wrong notes. The cheer squad make clumsy jumps, falling down, laughing. Some spectators squeal the obscenities they never shout during football games. When Sarena hits the high note, where "free" belongs, it's not the right note—it's one note below. I'm laughing by the time the performance finishes, but it's also kind of profound. Football is so ritualistic—there's something false about it. But this awful performance and the fight to follow . . . it's like the difference between a war story and a real war. The difference between a staged photo and a scared soldier.

The ragtag anthem ends, the dropped-pants sousaphonist waddling off last. Sarena returns to us.

"That was beautiful," says Iris.

The music achieved its intended effect—everyone's attentions are directed into the empty field. It's silent, flashlights flickering along the green.

"I hear them," says someone, and then I do, too.

In movies, armies always scream at each other as they approach the clash, psyching themselves up, but that doesn't happen here—maybe because the event is unsanctioned, or maybe for some other reason. The field is quiet as the two groups appear. Some players are still dressed in football jerseys, with the padding removed; others are in street clothes. Neither side is running fast—just jogging—but as they close in, I can see the adrenaline in their movements. It's true, I think, what Sarena said: none of them want this.

Then, quite unexpectedly, a voice booms out across the field. *"STOP!"*

I turn toward it, as does everyone. The teams halt their approach, confused, possibly relieved. They don't need to be told twice.

A figure steps from the shadows—it's Sylvester. He walks onto the field between the two groups. He isn't looking at either team, though they're all watching him attentively. Rather, he's focused on the visiting bleachers, the darkness. He holds up a hand and points. Flashlights follow his instruction, reaching across to the other sideline to illuminate the two shadowy figures there.

One of them I recognize immediately—Sylvester's father. I can see his pinned up coat sleeve. He's still dressed in his black suit from this morning, when I saw him in the protest. His hand holds a bouquet of red flowers—lotus blossoms.

The figure standing next to him I don't recognize. He is very, very tall.

The players on the field are as still as stones as the two forms make their slow way toward us, Sylvester's dad taking two paces for every one taken by the Death next to him, who moves through the thick currents of our air as a plow through heavy ground.

"Hercule," I whisper. I hope Iris hears me—I want her to know, but I find I can't raise my voice.

He's very thin, like all the Deaths, and silvery gray from his shiny dress shoes to his somewhat rumpled suit. His face is long, his expression tired, distant. Around his head float the thin wisps of his medium-length gray hair.

I scarcely know what I'm doing, but I find myself on my feet. I take Iris's hand, and then I'm rushing forward, past the transfixed audience, onto the field as Hercule and Mr. Hale reach Sylvester. I hear Sylvester's voice. He's crying. Iris clutches my shoulder, and I clutch hers. We've come as near as we dare, standing now among the statuary of the two terrified varsity teams.

Hercule extends one large gray hand.

Sylvester sobs more loudly, hopeless, then quiets himself. Finally, he reaches out.

He grasps Hercule's hand, and as his fingers close, he takes a deep, startled breath, and his eyes close. The color vanishes up the sleeve of his jersey, then from his neck and face. Within moments he is as gray as smoke. His hair lifts gently, moving in the newly buoyant air, and he exhales.

His lids flutter. He looks around, confused.

"It's over," says his father, his raspy voice cracking.

Sylvester releases Hercule's hand and looks down at his body. He turns to his father, who holds out the bouquet to him. Sylvester takes it, and the blooms turn gray instantly. Both father and son are crying, tears leaving brilliant tracks on their cheeks in the flashlight beams. They turn and begin to walk, approaching to within a few feet of Iris and me.

"Sylvester," I croak as he passes. He doesn't seem to hear me, but Hercule and Mr. Hale both turn. Mr. Hale, his voice measured and profoundly calm, says, "There's a wake tomorrow, at my home. You're welcome to attend." He says the address—maybe Iris will remember it.

Then, my eyes meet Hercule's. I see a glimmer of recognition. He knows me.

The group moves past us, continuing their slow walk toward the exit. Every eye is glued to them. Mr. Hale puts his hand on Sylvester's shoulder as they step into the shadows and disappear — toward the Fields.

The fight is over.

two days before
departure day

the wake

I'm not sure what time it is when I get home, maybe one
or two a.m., and I arrive to find Mom and Dad waiting for
me in the living room. They were called by both Iris's and
Sarena's parents. They know what happened. They're angry
and scared. I sit with them on the couch and tell them what I
saw — that Sylvester's Death was Hercule.

Dad wants to pray for Sylvester, and it seems like a good
idea. We close our eyes and fold our hands. Dad's words are
beautiful and heartfelt. He ends by saying, "May our will be
the same as yours, Lord," which is a common ending. Then
he adds, "May your will be the same as ours." He is thinking
about me — thinking about his desire for me to live.

After, Dad suggests that I should be grounded for attending the fight, but this suggestion is quickly taken off the table. It's clear that such punishments are meaningless to me

now, so we decide, sort of by consensus, that although I'm not grounded hopefully I'll feel a bit contrite about how much I made my parents worry. This seems reasonable, and the three of us, exhausted both physically and emotionally, hug one another and go to bed.

The next morning, an early phone call from the school informs me that all classes are canceled today—because of Sylvester's unexpected departure. Shortly after this, Iris calls, and about twenty minutes later I arrive at the Marking Street Café to find her seated by the window. We hug.

"Sylvester told me before," I blurt. "I wanted you to know, but he was keeping it a secret."

"Yes, well, did you ever kiss him?" she asks.

"Er," I say, "no. We . . . it almost happened. Out in the Fields, like Hercule said, but then it didn't. I'm glad, though." I say this with confidence, but I don't really know what I'm feeling on the subject.

Just then, Raahi and Sarena walk in, and we get down to business—the plan for the kidnapping tonight. Raahi will drive, and he'll pick everyone up around two thirty. I'll bring my Death Letter. Iris will bring the list of Hercule's former known departures. Sarena will bring the key to the back entrance of the Caballero. It is all arranged.

Then Iris says, "Do you guys want to go to Sylvester's wake? Mr. Hale invited us last night."

"I can drive us," says Raahi.

We pile into his car, outside the café. Iris and Sarena sit in back, and I take the passenger seat. Iris tells Raahi the address. We drive north.

Raahi is introspective, and I know what he's thinking about. "Tomorrow," I say, turning to him.

"Yeah," he agrees.

"Listen, Raahi, I have to tell you something . . . about my Wrap-Up List," I say.

Iris and Sarena both lean forward, pushing between Raahi's and my seats. This does not make things less awkward.

"What about it?" says Raahi.

"Um, you're on it," I say.

"Me?" He turns to me, taking his eyes off the road.

"Red light!" Iris observes. Raahi applies the brakes, and we come to a quick stop.

"Hercule's Hint wasn't very clear," I say, "but I think — for your item, that is — I think you need to be at the Caballero Wednesday night. I don't suppose there's any way for you to, um, get a deferment?" I ask. "Just for a day?"

"What did you put on your list?" Raahi asks.

"Green light," says Iris.

"I feel a little private about it," I mumble. Raahi isn't insistent. It probably doesn't matter anyway — so far my Wrap-Up List is a bust. Sylvester's departed. Raahi will be on a bus to Fort Jackson tomorrow morning. Iris . . . is complicated. It's all complicated.

· · ·

We enter Valley View Estates — a neighborhood of single-wide trailer homes. Some of the homes are rundown, with siding peeling off and rusting hulks of old cars in the yards. Others are meticulously kept, featuring fussed-over beds of petunias and gingerbread around the windows. There's a man unloading an old refrigerator from a hand truck, and an elderly woman drinking a glass of orange juice on a stoop.

"I wonder why Sylvester went to Central High and not North End," says Raahi. "This is really far from school."

Mr. Hale's house is obvious, because there are cars parked up and down the block from it, and the front door is open behind the screen door. His is neither the best- nor the worst-kept trailer in the neighborhood. The yard is a simple square of grass, brown and a little weedy. Raahi parks at the curb, and we walk the narrow cement path to the porch. I hear voices through the screen door, and the sound of a TV — a broadcast football game.

I knock, and a shadow disengages from inside. Mr. Hale approaches through the hall and opens the screen.

"Mr. Hale," I say, "we're all friends of Sylvester's."

"Hello, Gabriela," he says. He's still wearing his black suit from yesterday, with its pinned-up sleeve. His breath smells of whiskey. He steps across the threshold onto the porch with us, and I see that he isn't wearing any shoes — just black socks. He closes the door behind him and sits on the stoop. We sit, too. "Thank you for stopping by," he says. "Gabriela, I heard your news. When will you depart?"

"Midnight Wednesday," I say. "At the Caballero."

"I'd like to attend," he says. He looks at me intensely. "I know Sylvester told you. You and I were the only ones." He pauses, sighs. "Years ago, when I lost my arm, I thought I'd get used to it. But you never do. In fact, it gets worse with time." He rubs the stump through his coat, and a waft of acidic sweat floats past us. "I had to fight for him," he says, "all his life. Fighting to keep him during the divorce. Fighting to send him to the right school. Fight, fight, fight," he chants, bitterly recalling the football cheer. "Fighting to keep him from war."

"He wanted to volunteer," I say but don't offer anything else.

"Yes. I wouldn't allow it. When I think of myself as a kid . . . ah, just a damn *kid*." He shakes his head.

"I'm leaving tomorrow for basic training," says Raahi, suddenly.

Mr. Hale turns to him. "You volunteered, son?" he asks.

"No, drafted."

"What's your name?"

"I'm Raahi."

"They make it seem a fate worse than death, don't they, to refuse," says Mr. Hale.

"Refuse?" says Raahi. The word comes off his tongue as if it's from a foreign language.

"But consider this, son — at least it *is* a fate, and not death." Mr. Hale turns to me. "Perhaps you'll see him, Gabriela, out there in the Fields. If you do, tell him his dad loves him."

"I'm sure he knows that," I say.

"Remind him," says Mr. Hale. "You kids always need re-minding." He looks out across his patchy lawn and pulls a pack of cigarettes from his shirt pocket. He lights one with that economy of motion earned through years of practice. Inside the house, the announcer on the TV yells excitedly. Mr. Hale turns to Raahi. "To refuse," he says, punctuating his words with the lit cigarette: "To be a *coward*. And to have the opportunity to live with that." He throws the cigarette into the yard without taking a single draw on it. "Thank you all for coming," he says, standing. "I have to get back to my family now." Without another word, he returns inside. The screen door closes behind him with a clap.

I think about what Sylvester said—that he wanted to become a medic to finally impress his dad. To heap coals on his head. I could have told Mr. Hale just now, and I think it would have worked. But I'm glad I didn't.

My gaze drifts into the yard, where Mr. Hale's virgin cigarette sputters a final ribbon of smoke and goes out.

fidelia

As Raahi guides the car back toward our neighborhood, we're all quiet. I can tell from Raahi's expression that the conversation with Mr. Hale hit him hard.

"Turn left, Raahi," I say as we pause at an intersection. He obeys, going the opposite direction from our neighborhood. "I want to visit Abuela," I explain. "My grandmother's grave."

Raahi guides the car to Broadsprings cemetery, and we park in the lot. Iris and I lead the way. (She knows where we're going because we came out here together last year when we were doing an assignment on family histories, for Ms. Gulich. I took a rubbing from Abuela's gravestone to use as my visual aid. Maybe that was a little morbid, but it turned out to be one of the few assignments my freshman year that I did well on.)

We walk the well-maintained grounds, past the place where all the headstones read SMITH and HUXLEY, and past where they all read SONG and KIM, before reaching the neighborhood of our town's deceased Riveras. It's not surprising that things get grouped like that, I suppose. At one time, it may even have been required. These days I think it's more like what Dad says about our seating choices at Mass every week — "We sit with your aunt and uncle." Glancing at my friends now, though, I think I'd prefer to be buried in a mixed-up graveyard. Washingtons, Mehtas, and Van Voorheeses.

We find Abuela's grave looking well cared for. Dad comes here every Wednesday, and Aunt Ana every Saturday. There are fresh flowers in a vase, white daisies, which I'm sure Ana bought.

We stand silently around the headstone, which reads FIDELIA RIVERA.

"She never knew that her husband departed," I say. "She thought he was killed in action."

"I remember you saying you used to tell her stories about that," says Iris.

"Yeah — all kinds of crazy things," I say. "I remember one where Gonzalo jumped on a hand grenade. All the stories were about him being a hero." I kneel and gently place my hand on Abuela's stone, next to her name. I feel a little self-conscious, my friends watching me, but I continue anyway. I close my eyes and visualize her face, as well as I can remember it. She was a strict-looking woman who never smiled, but she was very kind. She taught me how to play lotería, which is kind of like bingo. I remember her being almost infinitely patient. "Hi, Abuela," I say. "It's Gabriela. I wanted to come tell you something. Maybe Dad or Aunt Ana already told you. We found out that Gonzalo didn't get killed in action. He departed!" I pause. "Maybe he told you that himself, if you guys are together now. I hope you're together. Oh, and if you think of it, could you ask Gonzalo what my Death's Noble Weakness is? I think he might know. Maybe you or he could tell me in a dream. It's okay if not. I hope everything is good for you, Abuela. I hope you and Gonzalo are happy. I pray for you every week at Mass. I miss you." I look up at my friends, who all seem respectful and a little awkward. I smile. "Anyone have anything they want to tell my grandma?" I ask.

"Hi, Abuela," said Iris.

"Hi," says Sarena, waving.

"Gabriela, are your mom's parents buried here, too?" asks Raahi.

"No, they're still alive somewhere," I say. "I don't know where. They disowned Mom when she married Dad."

"Oh, right," says Raahi. "I think you told me that. The . . . Martins, or something?"

"The Mason-Hunts. It's funny, all the ways people can go out of your life, huh? Abuela died from cancer. Gonzalo departed. And Mom's parents—they just opted out."

"I'm glad none of us are going to go out of one another's lives," says Iris.

"Me, too," I say.

the day before
departure day

the summoning

The apartment is dark at two thirty in the morning, when I wander into the perfectly still living room. It's as if no one has ever set foot in it before. I wonder if the whole world was like that, early on—an environment in which nothing had happened. Before God started making creatures. "On the third day, the LORD created two-bedroom apartments, and He saw that it was good. Next day, He created apartment dwellers."

I'm caught in a thicket of emotions as I make my way out—nervousness, guilt, hesitation, uncertainty. I ride the elevator, leave the building, and sit on the front steps waiting for Raahi.

Sneaking out is harder for Raahi than for me. He has to get past his mom, who is a very involved parent (and her only son is leaving for basic training in the morning). I imagine him pushing his car quietly down the block without starting it, so he's well out of earshot when he turns the engine over.

He's right on time to pick me up. We stop by Sarena's house next. She had it harder than either of us—she had to steal her dad's key to the back entrance of the Caballero.

We go to Iris's house last. She has it the hardest of all, because we're looking to her to get us through this.

Raahi parks in an alley behind the hotel. Sarena fumbles forever with the key at the back door, but finally we find ourselves standing, shivering (more from nerves than from cold) in a nondescript hallway dinged from countless collisions with countless musicians and staff people over countless decades. At a dim intersection, we turn right and step abruptly out onto the stage of the Caballero Restaurant.

I've seen Sarena play plenty of times with the Washington Fifteen, but I've never stood up here. Nor have I ever been in the Caballero at three a.m. It's a dark, silent cavern. There's no lighting at all beyond little dots of strung lights and a few spots shining on the walls, apparently always left on. The dance floor is a plot of empty boards. It seems impossible that a place this big would be completely, utterly empty. "Hello?" Iris says, her tiny voice ringing.

"Hello?" says Sarena, louder. *"Anybody here?"*

We climb down to the dance floor. The boards creak. I suppose they creak when people dance on them, too, but there's always so much other noise you can't hear it. The four of us stand, grinning stupidly at one another. Then Sarena says, "Hey, hold on a sec. Raahi, follow me."

She walks off the dance floor to the large circular dinner tables beyond, Raahi following. They reach the far wall and cross to the bar. Sarena places four shot glasses on the polished wood, selects a bottle from the shelf, and splashes liquor into each glass. She hands two to Raahi, takes two herself, and they return to us.

We clink the glasses together and drink. I've never tasted hard alcohol, and I think Iris hasn't either. While Sarena and Raahi swallow easily, we both sputter.

"What is it?" I say.

"Vodka," says Sarena.

Iris, still coughing, says, "I have no idea how this is going to go, you guys." She holds out a hand to me, and I give her my Death Letter. She places it in the middle of the floor. "Gabriela, you stand here, and the rest of us off to the side."

We follow her directions. Iris holds up the page she's working from, and explains: "This is the list of Hercule's known departures, from about seventeen fifty to, well — to yesterday," she says, showing everyone the sheet, which ends with "Sylvester Hale." "I'll read it, starting with the oldest."

"How long will it take, once we summon him?" says Sarena.

"Seconds . . . minutes? I don't know. I don't think anyone's ever done this," says Iris. Then she begins. "Anne Hawthorne," she says. She pauses to see if anything preliminary might occur. Nothing does. The room is silent. The dance floor gleams dully. "Fidel Guerrez," she continues. "Rita Heifitz. Henry Mallahan." She pauses again. I feel growing relief—maybe this won't work. Maybe we'll end up just a bunch of scared idiots.

"Itta Bernard," says Iris. "Chung Hee Sung."

"How many more?" whispers Raahi. It's funny that he whispers—none of the rest of us are whispering.

"Five, and then Gabriela," says Iris, and continues: "Amy Fuller. Regina McIntyre. Quincey Ibrahim. Gonzalo Rivera." She pauses. "Sylvester Hale," she says. We stand motionless. Finally, she says, "Gabriela Rivera."

Well, I'm ready to go home now, I think. *It's past my bedtime.* But then I must have blinked.

There's a chair in the middle of the dance floor, where no chair was before. It's upholstered in sparkly gray, with a low back. Carved claw-foot legs.

And seated on it is a very tall man. He's wearing a gray smoking jacket over an untucked dress shirt and dark, silvery slacks. His clothing floats aquatically around him. His legs are crossed, right ankle on left knee. In one hand he holds a gray glass of wine aloft, as if making a toast. He's smiling, his face raised, his eyes closed. His thin, gray hair floats over his head. I recognize him instantly—Hercule.

And the air is full of the merry tinkle of his laugh. He's right in the middle of something, which he probably began wherever he was when we summoned him. " —and so *I* said,

'Well, my dear, if that's what you want, I'm afraid I can't help you!' Haaaa-hahahaa!" His voice booms through the restaurant.

His smile fades quickly as he hears the silence around him. He freezes. His eyes flick open. He drops his glass, which bounces and then rolls across the dance floor. He stands, looking around in panic, and screams—a high shriek that pierces the air: "KIDNAP! KIDNAAAP!"

Before any of us can do anything, he runs. Like all Deaths, his movements look as though they're happening underwater. His loose jacket and slacks billow around him as he takes two large, slow strides, which deliver him straight to the wall at the left of the stage. He collides, rebounds, and falls onto his back, where he lies motionless. He begins to snore.

Raahi, terrified, whispers, "Is he dead?"

It would normally be pretty funny for someone to ask if a snoring person was dead, but no one laughs. Iris rushes forward. Of all of us, she's spent the most time around Deaths and is a little less starstruck. She rolls Hercule onto his side, and his snoring quiets. She looks up at us. "Help me tie him." She extricates a long coil of rope from her bulging purse.

Sarena comes to her aid as Raahi and I watch, fascinated.

"You brought *rope?*" I say.

Hercule is quickly secured from shoulders to feet. I finally get a good look at his face, which is long and pinched-looking, with a prominent silvery nose between the quotation marks of his little gill slits. As her denouement, Iris produces a black sleeping mask, which she places over Hercule's eyes. His thin hair floats, ghostly and weightless.

"Why a sleeping mask?" says Sarena.

"I don't know," says Iris. "It just seems like a good idea, right?"

Then Hercule speaks. We all jump as his voice booms out, not having realized that he'd regained consciousness. *"I wish to know,"* he says loudly, *"the identities of my abductors!"* His tone contains none of the panic that characterized it before. It's authoritative and angry.

"G-Gabriela Rivera," I say, voice quaking.

"Ah, *Gabriela,*" Hercule says. "A pleasure, I'm sure."

"We all did it," says Iris. "All . . . ten of us."

"That's right," says Raahi.

"You're surrounded," says Sarena.

"All *four* of you," says Hercule. He licks his lips.

I glance nervously at Iris, and see that her face is lit with triumph. She turns to me and whispers, "Time and venue."

"Hercule," I say, "I want to discuss my departure. When and where."

"What would you *like?*" he says, acidly.

"Midnight on Wednesday," I say. "Here, at the Caballero."

"Fine," he replies.

"Hercule," says Iris, "we want you to give Gabriela a Pardon."

"Of course you do," says Hercule.

"So," says Iris, "tell us your Noble Weakness."

Hercule doesn't respond right away. His broad mouth frowns. His shoulders straighten in their restraints. "Listen to me, *children*," he says distastefully. He takes a breath, and then intones, his deep voice inhumanly loud, resounding through the empty restaurant: "I am *Death!*"

Raahi begins stuttering, pushed by this into a kind of panic: "Right, certainly, okay, *yes sir* . . ."

Sarena puts both hands over her heart.

I look at Iris. Her triumphant expression is unchanged. She says, "There are some irregularities we'd like to discuss, Hercule."

"Like *what?*" he responds, a little frustrated that he didn't scare her, I think.

"Like, why was I on Sylvester's Wrap-Up List?" I ask suddenly.

Iris shoots me a surprised look.

"He showed me, the day I met him," I explain to her. "Hercule told him to wait for me."

"Wait for *you?*" says Iris. "You in particular?"

"For his Pardon."

"I hate to interrupt," says Hercule, "but that list is none of your affair."

"*Fine,*" says Iris, momentarily piqued at both Hercule and me. "Hercule, we also know you attended Gabriela's grandfather."

Hercule wiggles in his ropes. "These chafe," he says.

"Why have you chosen Gabriela?" she says. "Deaths never attend relatives of those they've already attended."

"Untie me, please," says Hercule.

"No. You might try to harm us."

"The longer you leave me trussed like an Easter ham, my dear, the more attractive such a proposition becomes," Hercule growls.

"My grandfather's Pardon was transferred," I say.

Hercule sighs. He stops wriggling. "It wasn't any use to him," he says.

"I don't understand," I say.

"I have no investment in that, young lady," says Hercule.

"Why are you being such a *prick?*" says Raahi suddenly. This comment completely derails the conversation. I see Hercule's surprise behind the sleeping mask. Then he smiles.

"Well, young man, I *apologize*," he says. "I shall reform myself and strive to be a more upstanding *prisoner*." He turns his masked face toward me. "The story of your grandfather, Gabriela, was not unusual in wartime. I arrived to find him seated alone at the base of an olive tree, suffering a bullet wound to the gut, delivered some time previous by an Italian rifle. He was dying when I took him, so you can understand when I say his Pardon was no use to him. He would return to life only to finish dying. So he decided to give it away."

"Oh," I say. This was a story I never thought to tell to

Abuela: Gonzalo giving up his own Pardon in his last moments of life.

"But he guessed your Noble Weakness," says Iris.

"Did you receive my response to your Wrap-Up List?" Hercule asks.

"Yes," I reply.

"Then you know everything I'm prepared to disclose on that subject." He snaps his mouth shut.

"Well, then, I . . ." I say. I glance at my friends to find them all looking at me expectantly. It seems silly to give up now—but I find myself feeling, suddenly, tired. Ready to go home. "You know what, Hercule," I say, "I guess I don't need anything from you. I'm sorry for the inconvenience. You can go back to whatever you were doing."

"You're sure, Gabriela?" says Iris.

"Yeah," I say.

"Very well, Hercule," says Iris, *"we dismiss you!"*

There's a moment of silence, and then Hercule seems to find something amusing. He giggles. Snorts. His mouth opens wide, showing his sharp, gray teeth, and he belts out a robust laugh. He rolls onto his chest and begins to guffaw into the floor. He hiccups and sniffles.

"What's so funny?" I say.

"Nothing," he replies.

"Hercule," says Iris, "how do we send you back?"

The question launches him into another torrent of hilarity.

This fit ends with a long, pleasurable sigh, and he says, "This is so much better than the party you took me from. I should thank you."

"Answer the question please," says Iris.

"My dear," says Hercule, "when a Death comes to collect someone, he does not leave until that someone is *collected*."

oatmeal

I open my eyes. I'm in my bed. My room is full of early morning light. Through the window, I see a pale blue sky with a few burnished clouds over the roof of the building across the street.

"Gabriela," says a voice. I don't recognize it. I squint into the shadows at the corner. There, sitting by my desk, is a tall old man. Very, very tall. His gangly legs, clothed in slate-colored slacks, are bent sharply at the knees. His head droops near the ceiling, and his face is long and thin. His little gills are tender gray at the sides of his prominent silvery nose.

The shreds of last night return—sneaking out of the Caballero with Hercule in tow. He wouldn't fit into Raahi's car, and I decided to walk back with him. Before we parted ways, Iris, Sarena, and I said our goodbyes to Raahi. We all hugged him. Sarena cried, and I thought Raahi was about to confess his feelings for her. But he didn't.

The bus to take him to Fort Jackson left at five this morning; he probably got home just in time to grab his bag. I imagine him on that bus now, duffel on his lap.

"Do Deaths sleep?" I ask, a little dizzy as I sit up.

"No, we do not," says Hercule, "so you can imagine how this situation has tried my patience. It is now morning, however, and I wish to go to Marking Street."

"To the café?" I say. "You don't need my permission."

"Nor do I desire it," says Hercule. A wisp of hair floats before his eyes, and he brushes it aside with his long, silvery fingers. "However, I require your *presence*. You and I are, for the moment, inextricable from one another."

"Inextricable?"

"Do you know that word, young lady?" says Hercule.

"Yes, I know that word."

"Well, it should fade with time. Deaths are compelled to be their most attentive on first arrival — typically the moment of departure. In this case, however, I've been summoned a bit early, *as you know*. Therefore, I must cajole your company."

I pull my hands across my tired face.

"Also," Hercule continues, "I've heard *noises*. I believe your father has left for work, and your mother is preparing breakfast. Is it her habit to awaken you? If so, you may wish to forewarn her of my presence."

That's a good point. I stand, and Hercule stands also.

"Exactly how close to me do you have to be?" I ask.

"Not sure yet."

We step into the hall and walk to the living room. The radio is on, playing music, and I smell cinnamon: Mom is making oatmeal. I motion to Hercule and whisper, "Stay back."

I enter the room alone, smiling to my mom, who's behind the kitchen counter.

"Good morning, honey," she says. "I'm making some —"

Then, with a lunge, Hercule springs forward from his concealment as if shot from a cannon, stumbling, clothes and hair swimming around him, his face frozen in an embarrassed half smile.

Mom screams — something I've never heard her do before. Then she plucks the pot of oatmeal from the stovetop and flings it at Hercule. It strikes him right on the forehead with an audible *bap*, and he careers to the side, into the sofa, and crashes down. Oatmeal everywhere.

I intervene as Mom rounds the kitchen counter with a meat cleaver in one hand. "Mom, this is *Hercule!*" I shout. "My Death!"

Hercule struggles to a sitting position, whitish clumps of steaming oatmeal rolling down his gray jacket and slacks. Mom slows her advance. Her fury dissipates as my words sink in.

"We summoned him so we could question him — Iris and I, and Raahi and Sarena," I explain. "Now he has to stay here until it's time."

Mom places the cleaver on the coffee table. She sits opposite Hercule on the disheveled couch. "Here?" she says.

"Um, yes," I say, looking around the apartment. "Here."

Mom nods, accepting this extraordinary circumstance with perfect calm. "Do you eat?" she asks Hercule.

"As a rule, yes," says Hercule, "though not generally oatmeal." He seems a little amused even as he rubs his forehead, where a bruise has begun. "However," he continues, "I have at the moment a pressing need to visit the Marking Street Café."

"Let's clean you up," says Mom. "I apologize, please understand . . ." Mom is a hands-on kind of person. She fetches a sponge from the kitchen and begins removing oatmeal from Hercule's clothes.

"Oh, totally unnecessary," says Hercule, holding out his arms so she doesn't miss anything.

When she's finished, Mom pulls on her coat.

"You're coming with us?" I say.

"I could use some coffee."

Hercule is a slow companion, pushing as he must with each step through our thick world. Mom offers him her arm, which he takes, laying his large gray hand on the sleeve of her coat. We stop at a few intersections to wait for the light, though there's no cross traffic — as if we're walking with a police officer.

We reach the Marking Street Café to find Iris sitting at an outside table, with tea and scone, her blond hair tied in a hasty bun. She looks worried when she sees us. She's hoping I'm not mad.

I hug her. "I'm not mad," I say.

"I had a feeling you'd come here," she says. "Hercule will want to gossip."

"The word is *discuss*," says Hercule.

"Alexandre and Dido are inside," says Iris.

"Can you go in without me?" I ask.

"I shall try," says Hercule, and he steps into the café, ducking his head under the lintel.

"He has to stay close to you?" says Iris, fascinated.

I nod.

"It's nice to see you, Mrs. Rivera," says Iris.

"You, too, Iris," says Mom. "And thank you . . . for wanting to help." Her tone suggests that although she's doubtful of the value of this help, she's touched by the intentions behind it.

Inside, Hercule stands before Alexandre and Dido. Alexandre wears a gray trench coat, and Dido a gray V-neck vest over her gray shirt. Hercule gesticulates, his smoking jacket wafting spectrally around him as he tells the tale of his abduction. I find myself embarrassed by him. What does it say about me that Hercule is appropriate to oversee my departure? All I have to go on is an obscure link between him and my grandfather. It's distressing that such an annoying, judgmental, presumptuous Death is drawn to my family.

He returns after a few minutes, holding a steaming cup of black coffee, which he places on our table. "Did you have a nice chat with your friends?" Iris asks.

"Those two," he says, "will inform my friends." He sits next to me, towering.

"Everyone who didn't hear your punch line?" I ask.

"Excuse me?" Hercule lifts one hawkish, silver brow inquisitively.

"Your punch line. When we summoned you, you said something about 'If that's what you want, I can't help you.'"

Hercule's face brightens. His large hands grip the edge of the table, and it shakes with his mirth. *"Priceless! Priceless!"* he cackles. "I vanished before their very eyes!"

When the volume of his joy diminishes, Mom says, quietly, "So — tomorrow."

"Your daughter has asked that I await the stroke of midnight," says Hercule, "which is a reasonable (and, I might add, *extremely common*) stipulation."

"Mom," I say, "are we going to have Tuesday Night Dinner tonight? I'd like to."

"Oh, yes — we can," she says. "I'll call Ana — " She cuts herself off. Then, without warning, she leaps to her feet. Iris's tea and Hercule's coffee go flying as she lunges at Hercule and grabs his jacket collar, shaking him. *"Grant her a Pardon!"* she yells.

"My! Good! Woman!" sputters Hercule, head bobbling, fingers pawing uselessly in Mom's iron grip.

She releases him with a defeated cry. No one is sure what to say, and we sit sullenly, our drinks drizzling to the ground.

"Iris and I can go get the groceries?" I say awkwardly. "Do you want, um, a roast?"

"Oh, you two don't have to — "

"I'd love to help, Mrs. Rivera," says Iris.

I glance at Hercule. He's straightening his smoking jacket. "Hercule?" I say.

"Hm?" He's brushing imaginary crumbs from his gray shoulders.

"Do you mind a little grocery shopping?" I ask.

He sighs.

"We'll walk to McPherson's, Mom, and meet you back home."

Then, from her purse, Iris unexpectedly produces a small point-and-shoot camera. "Mrs. Rivera," she says, "before we go . . . could I get a picture of the three of you? I thought, well — I don't know if you'd mind. But I was thinking, since this is all so unusual . . ."

"You're going to write an article?" I ask. "For the *Journal of Departure Science*?"

"I thought I'd try," she says.

"That's a *great idea!*" I say. In the midst of all of my own dilemmas, this seems even better than great. I immediately take an intense interest in staging the photo. I put my Death between Mom and me. "Hercule," I say, "you should smile, and Mom and I will look sad."

"No, I will not participate in this," says Hercule.

"*Come on,*" I say.

family dinner

Hercule, Iris, and I walk the few blocks to McPherson's. The appearance of Iris's camera has improved my mood — it feels good to help with something.

We roll our black shopping cart into the brightly lit produce aisle, where we're greeted by a seemingly limitless number of photographic opportunities. Such as that big crate mounded full of Red Delicious apples.

"Hercule, would you push the cart, and we could take a picture of you waiting while I choose apples."

"No," says Hercule, but he lays his hands on the handle of the cart. Immediately the whole black thing turns silver, like it's been dipped in paint.

"Does everything you touch do that?" says Iris.

"Everything I *grasp*," says Hercule.

"If you let go, does it come back?"

Hercule lets go, and the cart returns to black. "But not people, when it's their time," he adds. "If you two really want to see something, you should take a picture of me juggling. I can juggle four balls."

I almost laugh, but Hercule looks serious.

"Four *apples,* if you like," he says. He picks up four bright red apples, all of which immediately turn silver in his hands.

He begins to juggle them.

And it is amazing.

Not only does he effortlessly manage the apples, a feat in itself, but as soon as he catches one, it turns silver, and as soon as he tosses it, it turns red again. They wink red, silver, red, silver as they weave through the cascade of throws. Stranger still is that Hercule's movements, as always, are executed as if underwater, the wide sleeves of his gray smoking jacket billowing, his hands pushing against the thick air, but the apples fly normally in quick arcs. Back and forth. Red, silver. A crowd gathers. Two cashiers desert their stations to come and watch, and four or five people produce cameras before Iris remembers hers and finally snaps the photo.

When Hercule returns the apples to the crate, I say, "That was incredible!"

He is obviously pleased. "What's next on your shopping list?" he asks.

"The roast," I say. We head to the meat counter, where we take a great picture of Hercule browsing the various cuts.

• • •

Iris parts ways with us after shopping so she can go home and get her parents, and Hercule and I return to the apartment. Mom begins preparing the roast, and I decide to dress up. I head to my bedroom, Hercule trailing.

"Please stand outside the door," I say.

"I shall try," he says.

We manage this, and I commence examining the contents of my closet. I pull down a blue dress.

"So, do you have any questions for me?" Hercule asks idly from the hall, sounding bored.

"Well," I say, holding the dress before me in the mirror, "your Hints haven't been very easy."

"They aren't intended to be."

I place the blue dress on my bed and take out a red strapless, which I throw on quickly. My curly hair falls over my bare shoulders. It looks okay, but a little too much like I'm headed back to freshman prom. "I figured out the thing about *cavalier*," I say. "It's the Caballero. So I've invited everyone on my list. But Raahi won't be there — he left this morning, for basic training."

"Sorry to hear it," says Hercule.

"Also," I say, "Iris likes girls."

"She does?"

"I thought you should know, before you start Influencing things too much."

"Noted," says Hercule. Then, "Once you're at the restaurant, Gabriela, what do you intend to do to accomplish the items on your list?"

"Um, isn't that your department?" I say.

"You expect *me* to do everything."

"Well . . . yes?" I put the red strapless dress back on the hanger and replace it in the closet. I hold up the blue dress again.

"Certainly no one could request anything of *you*."

"Request anything?" I say.

"A cavalier request."

I drop the dress just as I pull it over my knees. "The song!" I say. I haven't given it a thought since all of this began—the lyrics I promised to write for Sarena, for her to sing at the Caballero.

When I enter the living room wearing the blue dress, Mom sees me from the kitchen. "You look *beautiful!*" she says.

"Thank you," says Hercule from behind me.

"Can I help with anything?" I ask.

Just then, there's a knock at the door. It's Sarena and Iris, with Iris's parents and Sarena's mother. Iris's parents look sort of like twins, both slim and well-dressed, with short blond hair. Sarena's mother is a large, tall woman with dark skin, hair braided similarly to her daughter's. She's smiling as she steps through the doorway with a platter of potato salad in her hands.

Then, the potato salad has been dumped on the floor. In the moment after, the caesar salad Iris's dad has brought also lands with a clang, lettuce erupting from the metal bowl. There's a scream, a shout, and everything is confusion. Croutons and square chunks of boiled potato scatter as Iris's parents and Sarena's mother panic at the sight of Hercule looming behind me.

I leap in to offer explanations, which doesn't help, because Hercule leaps after (as he must), and the next thing I know we're chasing our own guests down the hall toward the elevator.

Eventually, it gets sorted out. Everyone returns inside, and we all participate in the effort to clean up the mess and separate the scrambled salads. Iris's parents go into the kitchen while Iris and Sarena and her mom put the extra leaves in the dining room table under my supervision.

As the apartment fills with the scent of the roast, Dad enters, straight from work. He's dressed in a brown suit jacket and corduroy pants, and holds a platter stacked with frozen tamales, which he just bought at Central Carnicería. He smiles as he sees me, but when he sees Hercule he shouts, jumps, and drops the tamales, which clatter frostily across the parquet floor.

I leap forward, causing Hercule to leap forward . . . I could be doing a better job. In the hallway, I shout, "Dad, Dad! Didn't Mom tell you?"

Eventually, we retrieve him. Hercule says, "Pleasure to

meet you, Mr. Rivera." Dad crouches down silently to retrieve his tamales, a few long strands of his gray hair waving loose where they came undone during his panic.

He delivers the bruised tamales to the kitchen, and I hear him speaking sharply to Mom. "You could have *mentioned*," he says.

"Because I had nothing else to do today, you mean?" Mom replies.

I feel my ears growing hot. You know what—I've had enough of their bickering. I storm into the kitchen, dragging Hercule gracelessly behind me, and find them facing off before the stove.

"Quit it!" I say, sternly. Iris's mom and dad, who were arranging the tamales on a cooking sheet, turn demurely away as I scold my parents. "Why do you two always argue about *nothing?*" I say.

"I'm sorry, Gabriela," says Mom. "You're right."

"If you're going to act like children," I say, "I'm going to treat you like children. Now—apologize." I put my hands on my hips, and wait. Hercule, cramped against the kitchen ceiling behind me, also waits.

"Sorry, Grace," says Dad.

"I'm sorry, too," says Mom.

"Kiss and make up," I demand.

They kiss, a reluctant peck.

"Now *behave*. Dad, can I get you a beer?"

I fetch one from the refrigerator, and Dad, Hercule, and

I return to the living room and sit on the couch with Iris and Sarena and her mom.

Dad takes the band out of his hair. I've always liked it when his hair falls around his shoulders. It looks dignified. "Will you go to Mass tomorrow, Gabriela?" he asks.

"Yes," I say. I appreciate that he doesn't assume I'll go. He's really asking.

There's another knock at the door. It opens to reveal Aunt Ana; her husband, Hector; and Juan and Pia. They've made an enormous platter of sopapillas, covered with drizzled honey and powdered sugar.

In moments, it's on the floor, broken into pieces, globs of honey and puffs of sugar flying as Ana and Hector panic at the sight of Hercule. Ana recoils back through the doorway, carrying Pia and dragging Juan, and Hector bravely puts up his dukes.

I jump up and resolve things enough that everyone comes inside, and we begin the process of rescuing the pastries. Dad and Juan duck-walk good-humoredly around the entryway, collecting and stacking them in a tired-looking pile on the platter. I'm about to take it to the kitchen when there's another knock on the door. I look around the room—odd, I think everyone is already here.

Dad opens it, and as the unexpected visitors are revealed ... I drop the platter. The sopapillas take a messy bounce, flying again.

In the doorway stand Raahi and his mother, Charvi.

Iris and Sarena leap from the living room couch. *"How?"* says Iris. *"Raahi!"* says Sarena.

They enter. Charvi's wearing a navy blue sweater and gray slacks, and her shining black hair is piled copiously atop her head, fixed with two long green pins. It is her turn to be surprised when she spots Hercule. *"Great Scott!"* she says with her precise British accent. She's holding a pot of kheer, a dessert Raahi introduced me to, and fortunately manages to keep hold of it.

Juan takes charge of the recovery of the twice-dropped sopapillas, and the rest of us go to the living room, anxious to hear the story.

"What happened?" I ask Raahi.

"I decided not to go," he replies.

"And the Army was . . . *okay* with that?" says Iris.

"No, I don't think they'll be okay with it," he says.

"But what's going to happen?" I say.

"I'll be arrested, probably."

"Will you . . . um, go on the *run?*" says Sarena, clenching her hands in her lap.

Raahi smiles. "No," he says. He looks at his mom, and she puts one arm around her tall, skinny son. "Mom and I talked it over. We're just going to take what comes. Tomorrow, maybe, they'll find me. I want to thank you, Gabriela — it was talking to Mr. Hale that helped me make up my mind. I was already thinking about it, but after seeing him I knew what I had to do."

Juan has industriously recovered the sopapillas from the entryway, and he takes them to the kitchen. He returns now and, full of curiosity, sidles up next to Hercule and gives him an experimental poke with one finger.

"Juan, *no!*" says Aunt Ana, racing in. She grabs him away from Hercule, who smiles vaguely. So far, I'm thankful for Hercule's presence. I'd worried that he'd be a grim reminder of what awaits me at midnight tomorrow, but the opposite is proving true: the novelty of him distracts from it.

When the roast is ready, we gather around the table. We fold our hands, and Dad gives a blessing: "Dearest Lord, thank you for our family and friends, and for this opportunity to gather with them in your name. And thank you for our . . . special guests tonight. Everyone is welcome at the table of God."

The dishes are passed hand to hand. There's hardly any diminution of talk. It's almost like a regular Tuesday dinner. Hercule eats politely, and talks politely, answering questions and explaining common misapprehensions about Deaths — what they can and can't do. One major issue is the afterlife. Hercule explains that Deaths don't know if there is one or not.

"So, what do you do with people?" says Mom. "I thought you took them into the afterlife."

"We take them to the end of the Fields," says Hercule. "You call them the Oaks here, I believe."

"Fascinating," whispers Iris under her breath.

"Taking notes?" I ask. She nods.

"I've heard that departures are on the rise right now," says Aunt Ana, who has proven as curious about Hercule as her son, Juan.

"I wouldn't know," says Hercule. "I keep my own garden."

"Speaking of your garden," says Iris, "it's certainly strange to have you here while we're struggling with all of your Hints. Because you could just tell us."

"No, I can't," he says.

"Can't or won't?" she presses.

"Trust me when I say," he replies, "that these things are done as they *must* be done. There is no caprice in it."

"Hercule," says Ana, leaning forward. "I understand that you attended my father, Gonzalo."

Of course I knew this would come up, and yet it still surprises me.

"Sir," says Dad, "please tell us. I never knew him. My sister"—he gestures to Ana—"barely met him . . ."

"I'm honored to relate the story," says Hercule. He begins the tale he told me before, but as he proceeds this time, different details emerge. After explaining his arrival in the olive grove, and Gonzalo's mortal wound, he says, "My presence seemed to amuse him, in fact. There was a twinkle in his eye, you might say, that I haven't often encountered with souls on the verge of death. He struggled to his feet, despite his condition, and said . . ." Hercule pauses, and turns to me. "Do you speak Spanish, Gabriela?" he asks.

"No," I say.

"Well, he stood there, in his bloody uniform," Hercule says, "and said, 'Hello, sir. Welcome to my demise.' Isn't that wonderful? Shortly thereafter, he and I walked together to the Fields. As you all know, we Deaths become more active during war. It is not our pleasure, I assure you, but simply our nature. The day I departed with Gonzalo, there were others in the Fields, taking soldiers from all sides of the conflict: Italians, Frenchmen, Tunisians, Germans, Americans, Egyptians . . . It was astounding, so many former enemies walking together in the gray. Some were accompanied by loved ones, but most were alone. Gonzalo linked arms with a Tunisian soldier, a stranger to him. They did not even speak a common language."

"My daughter showed me a document the other day," says Dad, "which indicated that Gonzalo earned a Pardon."

"He did," says Hercule, "but it was useless to him. If he returned to life, he would have died within minutes from his injury. So he decided to give it away."

"This is real, then — the true story?" says Dad.

"Thank you," says Ana, who has raised her napkin to dab away tears.

Next, perhaps a bit bored with topics historical, little Juan asks Hercule if he has any funny stories. Hercule waves a hand to indicate a mountain of such stories behind him and proceeds to tell one about a particularly demanding departing woman. The tale ends with Hercule saying, "Well, my dear, if that's what you want, I'm afraid I can't help you!" Everyone laughs.

After the meal, we gather in the living room for broken sopapillas and coffee. As we eat, Dad stands and taps an empty wineglass with his fork. He's going to make a toast. Immediately, tears spring to my eyes.

"Everyone, everyone," he says. "Thank you for coming to this very special dinner tonight. You know, those things in life that matter most—"

I wonder what the rest would have been, if he could have finished. I imagine him working on the speech, writing it out carefully. But he delivers only these first words before his voice cracks. He stands perfectly still, his glass raised, lips trembling.

I go to him and wrap my arms around him. *"I refuse!"* he barks, at no one. *"I refuse!"* His fingers tangle in my hair. It is awful to be grieved.

writing

After the guests have all left and my parents have turned in for the night — after it is very late — I find myself alone with Hercule in my room. I'm at my desk, shoes off. He's next to the window, clothes and hair wafting gently.

"Your parents' makeup kiss was not very convincing," he observes.

"I agree," I say, thinking back on it.

"Do you think they could both use a good *first kiss?*"

I eye Hercule. "Are you making fun of me?" I say.

"Not at all," he says, in a way that makes me think he is making fun of me.

"You sound like you're making fun."

He shakes his head.

"Well," I say, "they've been harping on one another for a long time."

Hercule gazes through the window into the darkness outside. "I wonder if you have the energy to comply with your friend's request of you. There's not much time left."

"What's your Noble Weakness, Hercule?" I ask. "I'm not going to figure it out, you know."

"'Always about to disappear,'" says Hercule, and he snorts approvingly at the ingenuity of his riddling. "Pardons are such selfish things anyway, don't you think, Gabriela? And isn't your list an attempt to provide for others?"

"I guess so," I say.

"Don't sit on your hands now. You have a role to play. Start writing. You like to write, don't you?"

"I . . . I don't really know," I say. I pull a blank sheet of paper and a pencil from my top desk drawer while Hercule looks on disapprovingly.

"Don't give me a disapproving look right now, please," I say.

"I am not giving you a disapproving look."

"Yes, you are—you still are."

"Am not. This is my sad look."

"Sad?"

"That you're so young. You don't even know yet if you like to write." He pauses. "As to your difficulty getting started, let me say this: there's no answer but to try. Have you read Samuel Beckett? He once said, 'Try again. Fail again. Fail better.'" Hercule closes his eyes. When he opens them, he says, "Let me tell you a little more about your grandfather's death. Something I didn't reveal during dinner, which is simply this:

When I first met Gonzalo in the olive grove, he stood and greeted me as I said, but he did one other thing as well. He recited a poem, which was dedicated to his family."

"He wrote poetry?" I say. "Do you remember it?"

"It was like a prayer, and there was a general principle to it that might be of use to you. He wrote about the people he cared about." Hercule pauses and looks out my window again, down on the lamplit street. "Your father does the same, doesn't he? He writes prayers for people in your church." Hercule reaches out and cracks open my bedroom window. "Think of someone you care about," he says.

A waft of cool air enters through the crack. And riding upon it is the strong smell of flowers — the very smell that's been my intermittent companion all week. I breathe deeply. Hercule does, too.

"They're hydrangeas," I say.

"They're *hyacinths*," he replies.

"Hercule," I say, "your Hint, about my first kiss. You wrote 'The Fields.' But Sylvester and I went there and it didn't happen."

"You have a complaint?" says Hercule.

"No, just . . . an observation, that it didn't work out."

"Wrap-up items do not always work out," says Hercule. "I'm not a magician, you know."

"But I thought you were," I say. "I thought you could make things happen."

"I can only encourage things that *might* happen. For instance, some events with relevance to your Wrap-Up List *might* transpire tomorrow night at the Caballero, given the correct circumstances."

The smell of the flowers reminds me intensely of that day — Sylvester and I. I find myself wishing for him . . . wishing for another try at that kiss. He messed it up, but maybe he'd do better with a second chance.

I pick up my pen.

I write.

departure day

ash wednesday

A dream: I'm in the living room of the apartment, watching TV with Mom. It's a report about the war, and we can see the troops marching while the announcer describes it. Then fighting begins, and it's impossible to say what's happening — war is too complicated for television. Who's a good guy and who's a bad guy becomes hopelessly confused. I creep close to the screen, trying to understand, and a stray bullet flies out. I'm struck in the chest and knocked backwards onto the carpet.

I sit up to find Dad watching me from the couch. "You're dead," he says.

"No, I'm not," I reply.

"Are you hungry? If you're hungry, you're alive."

In fact, I am hungry. Ravenously hungry.

"Gonzalo dropped an olive around here somewhere. I wonder if we can find it," says my dad.

On the radio, the war is over. The speakers hiss. I look for Dad, but he's disappeared. Hercule is there. He holds out a silver hand.

My last day begins with me shutting off my alarm clock. I sit up tiredly in bed and swing my legs to the floor in the half darkness of the room.

"Good morning," says Hercule from by the window.

I stand and walk into the hall, Hercule following closely. As I move to shut the bathroom door, he's right there, halfway through. *"Really?"* I say. This hasn't been a problem before, but apparently it is now.

"If it's any consolation," says Hercule, "I will close my eyes."

Grumpily, I allow him in, and he stands by the wall as I pee.

"You have a powerful stream," he observes.

"Thank you," I say. I can't believe this is my first conversation of the last day of my life.

The sun has just risen as my parents, Hercule, and I walk to church. I observe my surroundings closely: the redbrick building across the street, newspaper boxes by the light pole, parallel-parked cars, light glancing from windows, grass blades creeping through cracks in the sidewalk . . .

We reach St. Mary's to find it decked soberly for Lent. Instead of taking our usual seats in the transept, we stand at the back of the nave, not wanting Hercule's presence to cause a stir. As it is, we get plenty of curious, stern, and fearful glances. The church is solemn and quiet. The congregation looks tired, and I know some people are fasting and keeping vigil during these days.

I've always liked Ash Wednesday. I imagine that this service alone is still like it was at the very beginning of Christianity. No matter where you live, or when, whether you're a modern person or a historic one, death is sad.

The service includes somber readings and singing. Father Ernesto gives a short homily. He's got more on his mind than the fact that I'm departing today, but his words seem meant for me. He speaks of preparations, of the repentant attitude that should be with us through Lent, and of the sorrow of our physical demise. Our spiritual immortality, he says, does not exempt us from the tragedy and pain of death. Indeed, in the Bible, Jesus weeps when Lazarus dies. But Father Ernesto can't help letting in a ray or two of light as well. How can you not, when you know Jesus will come back? Despite the awful, cold certainty of it all, the mind makes that leap of faith. To jump for a wild pass you can't possibly catch. *At least it is a fate, and not death.*

At the conclusion of the service, a line forms down the central avenue from the altar to the front doors, where several deacons stand with bowls of ashes. These they apply in the shape of a cross to the forehead of each person. Everyone leaves marked. When Hercule reaches the front of the line, the person making the crosses is speechless and afraid. Hercule says, "Don't worry if I'm too tall to reach."

We return to the apartment afterward, the sun shining brightly between buildings. It's going to be warm, probably the warmest day so far this year. Sarena, Iris, and Raahi are waiting for us on the front steps.

"Raahi!" I say.

"Still here!" he says cheerfully.

"Will you come to the Caballero tonight?" I ask.

"They'd have to drag me away," he says.

We walk up to the apartment. Mom tosses her purse on the kitchen counter and says, "Anyone hungry?"

"Kind of," I say. "Are there any leftovers from last night?"

"You want *leftovers?*" She laughs, and I do, too. I really do want leftovers, though. She goes into the kitchen to begin heating them up, and I turn to Sarena.

"Sarena, I wonder if I can show you something."

"Sure," she says.

We leave Iris and Raahi, and go to my room, followed by Hercule.

"I don't want those guys to know," I say. "Maybe it's silly, but . . . well, I wrote you some lyrics. For your song." I take the page from my desk. "I don't know if they're any good. They're probably not. But . . ." I hand it to her.

She reads, and I twist my fingers together.

After what seems an eternity, her eyes reach the bottom of the page. She smiles. "They're *great,*" she says. She places the page on the desk and picks up a pencil. "It fits almost perfectly! I'll trim one line . . ." She starts scribbling in the margin. She looks over at me. "Gabriela, I'm going to perform this. The band already knows the tune."

"Perform it . . . *tonight?*" I say.

She folds the sheet, puts it in her pocket, and gives me a hug. "Thank you," she says.

snake lake

Mom heats up lunch, and we all eat together. With each bite, I'm aware of time passing. The leftovers disappear with distressing speed. *This is really it*, I think, *my last day*.

Mom and Dad take the plates into the kitchen and start loading the dishwasher. I look at my friends. "You guys," I blurt, "do you want to go for a drive?" Because that's what I want all of a sudden — to get out of town for a few hours.

"Where to?" asks Raahi.

"How about Snake Lake?" I say. "We'll come back in time to go to the Caballero."

I break the news to my parents, and they accept it though I can tell it grieves them to think of spending time apart from me today. It grieves me, too, but a few minutes later Iris, Sarena, Raahi, Hercule, and I pile into Raahi's car. Raahi and Sarena are in front, and Iris and I are in back with Hercule sandwiched between us. That first night, when we thought Hercule couldn't fit into this car? We just didn't try hard enough. He's crammed, shoulders between his knees, head jutting forward.

Though Raahi's car has no radio in it, we have Sarena, who's a human jukebox. As the car climbs out from town, she leads us through a hit parade of today's Billboard toppers. In about twenty minutes, we're entering the pines. At the Y that leads left to the Fields or right to the lake, we go right. The city falls picturesquely behind and below, cut by the blue ribbon of the Snake River. Its source is the lake we're heading for, Snake Lake, near the top of the foothills, a popular day trip with plenty of private nooks because of its circuitous shape.

"Hey, Gabriela, remember this one?" says Sarena, and she starts singing a song I'd almost forgotten:

> *Caro mio ben,*
> *credimi almen . . .*

"Did you hear that guy sing it?" I ask. "The Singing Man?"

"You just listen once, and you remember it forever?" says Raahi.

"I don't have an eraser when it comes to music," says Sarena, then continues, *"senza di te languisce il cor . . ."*

We enjoy our first glimpse of Snake Lake. It isn't particularly amazing, because you only see one bend at a time without ever seeing the whole thing, but what's visible at the moment—bright blue water reflecting the blue sky—satisfies me that I picked the right thing to do for the afternoon.

The first parking lot has cars in it already, so we drive to the next, and then to the third. At the fifth little lot, there's no one. We park and step into the sunshine. I stretch and turn my face skyward, eyes closed, thankful for this unseasonably warm day. Everyone follows suit except for Hercule.

"Hercule, doesn't the sun feel good?" says Iris.

"I don't feel heat," he says.

"You don't feel the sun?" I say.

"No."

"Can you get a sunburn?" says Iris.

"We can neither burn nor freeze."

We all fall silent at this. I can tell everyone feels it — just in case we were about to start looking at Hercule like he was a regular person, these little facts keep emerging. *We can neither burn nor freeze.*

The part of the lake we can see from our private waterfront is very nice, a long watery hall lined with boulders and protruding stumps. Snake Lake is an odd place — there are dead trees sticking out of it, as if they grew up through the depths. They're a hint that this lake is man-made. Decades ago, before my parents were born, there was no lake here — instead, there was a town called Andeola, a tiny spot with a few hundred residents.

The people living down in the valley decided they wanted electricity. One good way to get it was to dam the Snake River just below Andeola. So the valley bought out the town, over the course of about ten years, and all the residents relocated. Then the dam was built. The river swelled, and Snake Lake grew, swallowing Andeola. The town is still down there somewhere, abandoned, empty, and nearly forgotten. Every once in a while something breaks free from the bottom and floats up. Last year a toolshed appeared, with tools still in it. Because of some initials carved into the remarkably preserved handle of a rake, the Municipal Archives (with my dad's help) deduced the former owner and located the grandkids, now elderly men and women, who donated it all to the county museum.

Most of the time, though, you don't see anything. On a sunny day like this, with the water the color of bluebells and emeralds, it's strange to imagine the dark, silt-covered town below.

Because of the nature of the lake, there aren't sandy beaches here. The water's edge is composed of hillsides and boulders. The spot we've chosen today is one we've all been to before. We ascend a large boulder to its flat lookout. The rock is warm from the sun. We throw blankets onto the sunny sandstone and relax. Hercule wanders the top of the boulder, looking around a little — the tether between us, at the moment, is slack. Eventually he sits as well, first fussily dusting off a little landing zone for himself.

After reclining for a few moments, Sarena stands. She takes her wallet out of her jeans pocket. She takes off her watch, and her shoes and socks. Then she steps to the edge of the boulder, a cliff about fifteen feet above the surface of the lake. Her face shines in the sun streaming over the hilltops. We know what she is going to do.

She looks back at us and shouts, "Cannon-ball!" She leaps over the edge, and disappears. There's a brief silence, then a splash, and then a series of cold-inspired shrieks. We listen to her paddle to the base of the boulder. She climbs out and hurries back to the top, sending chilly drips onto everyone. She towels off, briskly rubbing her now-soaked clothes, and then flops down to start drying off. "Warm as bath water out there," she lies.

Raahi stands next. He takes off shoes and socks, and continues to strip down to his surprisingly flowery boxer shorts. I haven't seen him dressed to swim since we last came up to Snake Lake, last summer. He's changed a lot. There's hair on his chest that wasn't there before, and his body, which was bony and angular last year, has filled out. He looks graceful as he approaches the edge, surveys the drop briefly, then bends his knees. He leaps high and disappears in a graceful dive. "Wow!" I say as he goes. There's a quiet *snik* as he slices into the water.

"Fairly good," says Hercule, "though he overextends his arms."

A few moments later, Raahi returns to the top of the boulder, dripping.

"Where did you learn to do that?" says Iris.

Instead of replying, Raahi dives again. When he returns

this time, he says, "You guys have never seen me dive? That's weird. I used to be pretty good for my age group." He towels off. Maybe the lake really is as warm as bath water—it doesn't seem to have bothered him.

Iris takes off her shoes and socks, and then strips to her underwear—black bra and panties. She's always been the most mature of us, but like this, poised before a whitish blue sky in the brisk snap of the spring air, she looks like a model in a magazine with long, slender arms and strong legs. She jumps, taking a straightforward approach. A few moments after the splash, she climbs back up . . . and it's my turn.

I take off my shoes and socks. Following Iris's lead, I disrobe to my underwear. I step to the edge and look down. The water is glassy and clear in the shadow of the boulder, but all I can see through that clearness is the silt that stands suspended through it, a wafting field of greenish gray.

"Go, Gabriela!" says Sarena.

All of them are sitting behind, pushing at me with their eyes. *Go.*

I jump.

The journey from the rock to the surface of the lake is so brief that calling it a journey is an overstatement. It's an interval.

The lake and I collide, and the freezing water engulfs me—a tiny bit of nothing thoughtlessly swallowed. My eyes pop open and confront the fuzzed, steady wall of silt. Below me somewhere is the abandoned town of Andeola, held eternally among the shreds. Old fence posts. Empty kitchens.

Then the lake seems to say, *Not yet, Gabriela.* It pushes me upward, ejecting me into the sun accompanied by a shower of glittering droplets, to see my friends smiling down from above.

When I return to the top of the rock, Iris reaches out and puts her thumb on my forehead.

"What are you doing?" I say.

"Your cross is running," she replies.

"My cross?" I'm not sure what she means. Then I remember—the ash cross I got after Mass. I'd forgotten about it.

Sarena approaches with a handkerchief in one hand, and Raahi with his shirt. They all go to work, rubbing my forehead clean. Behind them, Hercule stands and watches. His long shadow falls over us.

always about to disappear

I don't know where the day goes, exactly. Where does life go? The questions are the same.

Iris, Sarena, Raahi, and I are all in my living room. We're dressed up. Iris wears a white shirt with a white knee-length skirt over green stockings (she looks like the flower she's named after). Raahi has on a blue shirt with a wide collar, and tan pants that reveal about an inch of his yellow socks. Sarena is in her suit—her uniform for the Washington Fifteen. I'm wearing my blue dress from last night (I can't help that it's my favorite). All four of us are sitting on the couch, Hercule on a chair across from us.

"Okay, we're ready!" I shout, and my parents emerge from the hall to take a slow turn. Mom's wearing a long green dress with a white cardigan, and Dad's in a light brown suit with a matching vest, which must have come from a spot in his closet he hadn't plumbed for years. His hair is loose over his shoulders.

"You guys look great!" I say. It's true, especially with the evening sun streaming through the windows, but I can tell by the way they stand together that they still haven't made proper amends. Maybe they're past such things now. Maybe at some point it's impossible. Nonetheless, they're making an effort, and I appreciate that.

"Should we take two cars?" I ask.

"I'll drive us all," says Dad.

"Your car?" I say, envisioning his old station wagon, filled to the ceiling with boxes.

It's parked at the curb right outside. And for the first time in my memory it isn't crammed with junk. Also, it's been washed and waxed. The wood paneling shines, and the hubcaps gleam.

"What did you do with all the . . . stuff?" I ask.

"The dump," he says.

Despite the incredible spaciousness of the emptied car, we're in close quarters: Mom and Dad in front; Iris, Raahi, and Sarena behind; and I and Hercule in the rear, in the seats that face backwards—it's the only place where Hercule can fit. As Dad begins to drive, Hercule and I watch where we've been.

Sarena's dad has been playing music at the Caballero for as long as I've known Sarena. His job as bandleader was the reason her family moved here. Although our city is small potatoes compared to Chicago, the Caballero is a nice hotel.

We enter through the large double front doors and walk past the lobby to the restaurant. It looks considerably different from when I was last here (at three in the morning). The stage at the front is set with risers and chairs, occupied already by the band's instruments. Before it, the smooth boards of the dance floor shine in the red and yellow stage lights. Ranged around this area is the restaurant seating, large circular tables. Because it's early, I don't expect to see many people, but a quick glance surprises me. There are lots of people here, and I think I know most of them. At one table I see Ms. Lime sitting with two pear-shaped children whom I take to be her sons. Near the dance floor, Wendy converses with some kids from school—Dawn Fuller and Meg Rhinehardt (both cheerleaders) and Milo Stathopoulos and Jeff Dounais (from the football team). It seems like word got around.

At another table I see Aunt Ana with Hector and the kids, all of them eating plates of spaghetti. Another group enters behind us—it's Iris's parents and Raahi's mother.

Dad tells the maitre d' the name for our reservation, and we're led toward our table, near the dance floor. I'm still gawking at how many people have showed up when suddenly I feel a tugging in my chest. It's like my insides are being yanked backwards. I press on, but the sensation increases. I turn around.

Behind me, Hercule has stopped walking. He's standing

stock-still at the edge of the dance floor, peering intensely across the restaurant at the far wall. I try again to move forward, and again am prevented—it's definitely Hercule, standing stiff and resisting the pull of me. He fixes me with a glance and says, commandingly, "Come here!"

I obey out of curiosity. He points to the far end of the restaurant. "There," he says, with a smug satisfaction that indicates he thinks he's proved something.

"What?" I say. I look out across the tables, full of friends and acquaintances.

"There!" he says again, shaking his pointing finger. "I know you see it."

"It?" I say.

"Yes, *it*," says Hercule. "My *chair*. From my *house*. You summoned it with me, and this restaurant has now stolen it."

Hercule wades in through the tables, me hustling to keep pace with his long, slow strides. He causes considerable commotion, people craning their necks or leaping from their seats as he passes.

We reach the chair, and I do remember it—low back and seat upholstered in sparkly gray, carved claw-foot legs. Hercule lifts it with some difficulty and drags it from the wall. We make our return journey to our table, my parents and friends all watching with great interest. When we reach them, Hercule says, *"My* chair," as he puts it down. He gives the maitre d' a challenging look, and the man holds up his hands and backs away. Hercule sits in his chair, and the rest of us sit in ours. We're informed of the specials, which I don't listen to — I'm still looking around. I see Mr. Hale. I see Father Ernesto and Father Salerno.

My long glance ends at the stage, where it encounters, above the risers on the back wall, a clock. It's nothing fancy — a round metal clock like in our classrooms at school, with bold black numbers. As soon as I see it, my gaze is pinned. It shows five after seven. It ticks insistently.

"Good to see all of you."

I pull my eyes from the clock when I hear Sarena's dad's voice. He's a large man, wider and taller than my dad, wearing a black suit with a trumpet lapel pin. I wonder if Sarena will eventually prove to have the same body type as her dad. It's kind of funny to imagine her as a giant forty-five-year-old. I glance across the table at Iris and Raahi. How will they look when they're our parents' age? Rounded, wrinkled. Happy, I hope.

Sarena's dad has always struck me as easygoing, though Sarena says he has a temper. But he loves his work, and if Sarena sticks with music, she'll have a career she loves, too. "Gabriela, it's especially nice to see you," he says.

"I'm looking forward to hearing you play," I say.

"Everything is on the house for this table tonight," he announces, "courtesy of the band." He gestures to the empty risers as if the band were there, tipping their hats to us. My eyes flick back to the clock above the stage. Two minutes have passed during this exchange. I feel cold.

Sarena and her dad depart backstage, and the rest of us study our menus, then place our orders. Dad requests a bottle each of house white and red for the table. I ask for the tuna tacos. Hercule requests an extra-rare rib-eye steak. "And when I say extra-rare," he explains to the waiter, "I'd like the chef to simply *consider* cooking it."

Soon the band enters the stage, everyone in suits. When Sarena steps out, our whole table shouts her name. The band members file onto the risers and take up their instruments — trumpets, saxophones, trombones, a bass guitar, and drums. There are fifteen people including Sarena's dad, who leans over a mike at the front and says, "I'm Clyde Washington, and we're the Washington Fifteen."

They begin to play. The music is up-tempo, the trumpets bright and fast. I glance at Hercule to see his reaction. He's leaning back in his chair, face tilted toward the ceiling. His eyes are closed, and he nods along. When I first met him, I couldn't have cared less what kind of time he'd have tonight, but I find myself glad he's enjoying it. Aggravating as he is, I guess he's growing on me.

An enthusiastic audience takes to the dance floor. Raahi stands next to my chair and offers me his arm. He knows I don't know how to dance, and I know he doesn't know how. We walk onto the gleaming floor as the band begins a slightly slower number. The people around us are doing some step I don't know — jitterbug? Foxtrot?

"Thanks for spending today with me," I say.

"I'm honored," says Raahi. "You're one of the best people I know, Gabriela. Everyone thinks so, actually."

"They do?" I say, raising a skeptical eyebrow.

"But you aren't conceited about it."

"Oh-kay," I say, grinning despite myself. Onstage, Sarena takes a solo. She isn't quite as polished as some of the other performers, but she's also less than half their age. I like seeing her up there.

"So," I say, moving the conversation away from my merits, "has anything happened? About, you know, not reporting for duty?"

"There was a call," says Raahi. "My mom took it. They asked where I was, and she said I was at home, and that I didn't intend to comply with the draft. They're sending MPs tomorrow. They'll arrest me, I think."

"Oh, my God," I say.

"I'm glad," he says. "Everything that's happened in the last week, everything with Sylvester, and Mr. Hale, and even you putting me on your Wrap-Up List . . . it all helped me. I know I made the right decision."

"How long will you go to jail for?"

"I guess a judge will decide," says Raahi. "I'm going to say I'm against the war. But I want you to know," he says firmly, "that I *owe* you . . . I probably owe you my life." When the song ends, we return to the table. The soup and wine arrive. I ordered lentil soup, and I see Hercule has the same. He brings a spoonful near his mouth and holds it by his gills. He takes a sip.

The band plays two more fast numbers, and the floor crowds. Dad serves wine, walking around the periphery of our table. He gives me a little more than everyone else. "How are you doing?" he asks, tousling my hair.

"I'm okay," I say.

Soon, distressingly soon, the main course is delivered, and the stage clock's hour hand continues its slow climb. Nine o' clock: I'm popular on the dance floor. My parents each ask me for a song, and Wendy comes over from her table and asks after that. Father Salerno even takes me for a turn — and he's an excellent dancer. He says he used to dance competitively. I'm not surprised. *I understand how things are now,* I think.

Ten o' clock: Dessert is served, and I eat a scoop of orange sorbet. Then, I sense Hercule standing next to me.

"I recall asking, early on," he says, "if you would save me a dance." He towers overhead, his grayish silver form spectral in the stage lights.

Then, from the side, Iris says, *"Smile!"*

Hercule and I turn to find her peering at us through the lens of her camera. The flash goes off.

"Me, just before my departure," I say.

"I'll title it 'Gabriela About to Disappear,'" says Iris. No sooner are the words out of her mouth than both of us gasp, astonished.

"The Hint!" we say in unison. It was right in front of my nose the whole time: the photo of Grandfather Gonzalo. On my desk. There he is, preserved a moment before he was lost forever — *always about to disappear.*

I turn to Dad, holding out one hand. *"Car keys!"* I command him. He takes them unquestioningly from his pocket and is about to give them to me when something quite unexpected occurs.

There's a couple standing nearby, an elderly man and woman. They've been here all evening, dressed in fine clothes — the man in a suit, and the woman in a long, black dress that curves over her hunched shoulders. I've seen them a few times, eating at a distant table. But now they are right here. They've approached us for some reason.

And when Dad sees them, his whole demeanor changes. His face goes pale, and in his eyes is a kind of rage that I've rarely seen him display — so intense that all of the good humor in him is burned up by it.

Then Mom is at his shoulder, placing one firm hand on his elbow.

"José," she says, using his first name calmingly.

But her tone does nothing to stanch the force of Dad's anger. *"You!"* he says loudly to the couple. He takes a step forward, aggressively. "How dare you!" He points at them and repeats, louder: *"How dare you?"*

I think he might actually take a swing at these people. My mind is reeling, and my desire for the car keys is forgotten.

"Get out of here!" Dad yells, waving his arms toward the doors. The old couple backs off, and Dad turns to Mom. "Did you *invite* them? Did you *bring* them here?" He's out of control. I've never seen anything like this before, and I stare, transfixed.

"I wanted them to see her," says Mom quietly. "And now they have. Now they'll leave."

Finally, I understand. These are the Mason-Hunts — Mom's parents. My grandparents.

The scene is a paralyzed tableau in which my grandparents haven't quite left, my dad hasn't quite attacked, and my mom hasn't quite calmed anyone down. But one person is not caught up in it — Iris. She darts forward, snatches the car keys dangling from Dad's fingers, turns, grabs me, and shoves me toward the exit. "No time!" she says. And then I'm running with her. I think I hear Hercule's voice yelling after me, but I'm moving too fast to listen.

first kisses

Outside, Iris and I jump into Dad's car. She gets behind the wheel (she's been taking Driver's Ed at school this quarter), and we roll into the street.

"What was that all about?" she says, accelerating through a yellow light, going kind of fast.

"My mom's parents," I say. "I've never seen them before."

Iris leans forward, her chin nearly touching the steering wheel as she speeds toward my apartment building. "*Faster,*" she whispers to the car.

In a few minutes, my block appears before us, the old square brick buildings forming walls to either side of the street.

Then, out of nowhere, I feel a sudden, violent pull in my gut—it's like someone's trying to rip me right out of myself. "Oo-*wowh!*" I say. The force of it yanks me backwards into my seat, and I'm pressed there, pinned as the car races on.

"What? What?" Iris shouts, swerving.

I can't speak. I feel like I'm being crushed by a hundred gravities. I've got one hand on my chest, the other on my abdomen, and they each seem to weigh a thousand pounds.

Iris hits the brakes and screeches to a halt in the middle of the street. "It's Hercule!" she says. "Your connection to him—we stretched it too far!"

My head is locked against the headrest. My feet are pulling backwards, wedged under the seat. *". . . get . . . the . . . picture . . ."* I whisper, though my tongue is straining back the way we came, and my lungs are wrapped around my shoulder blades.

Without another word, Iris opens her door. "The photo on your desk, right? Of Gonzalo?"

I can't reply, but I manage to creep my fingers into my purse and produce the keys to the front door.

Iris takes them and rushes down the block while I sit, paralyzed. The moment I'm alone, everything seems very quiet. There are no cars on the street. No people. I watch Iris climb the stairs of the apartment building and slip through the front doors. I look into the rearview mirror, back down the empty street. *Always about to disappear,* I think. I feel like I should make some important realization as I sit here with nothing to do, but I don't realize anything except that this really, really hurts.

Finally, Iris bursts back through the front doors and rushes to the car with the framed photo in her hands. She holds it before me. Turns it upside down. "What is it? What is it?" she says.

"Take it out of the frame," I whisper. I try to lift my hands to do it myself, but they're too heavy.

Iris releases the little catches around the edge and pulls the picture free. Together, we look at the back of it. There's writing on the old, yellowed photographic paper. Two lines, scrawled in an awkward cursive. In Spanish.

"What does it say?" says Iris.

"I don't know," I moan. "But . . . Dad can translate."

Iris starts the engine and executes a clumsy three-point turn. On the first point, the weird gravity that's pulling me toward Hercule slams me against the door. On the second point, I'm slammed against Iris, knocking her nearly out of her seat. She manages to get her hands back on the wheel and her feet on the pedals. I'm thrown forward against the dashboard as we speed back toward the restaurant. It's almost like my own body is pulling the car.

The pressures upon me lessen as we hurry on, and soon I'm sitting normally, freed—back within the bounds of an acceptable proximity to my Death. "Thank God," I say, breathing easily again, my tongue back in its regular place, my feet in theirs, and my organs in theirs.

"It's going away?" says Iris, looking worriedly over at me.

"Stop! Stop!" I yell, pointing ahead.

Iris slams on the brakes—as Hercule's giant and completely unexpected form looms up before us in the middle of the street. The car screeches to a halt.

I open the door and leap out. *"Hercule!"* I say. "What are you doing out here?"

He doesn't reply. His hair is a mess, floating in wild wisps. His smoking jacket is torn open, with the belt dangling, and his pants have holes in both knees, showing the silver flesh of his legs.

"I *distinctly recall,*" he says, *"yelling* after you. But did you listen? Did you stop?"

I'm trying to piece this all together. Hercule's dress shirt is askew on him, bunched up to reveal an iridescent belly button. "I felt a tug," I say, "as we were driving . . ."

"I'm sure you did," says Hercule. "The tug of me *flying from my chair.* The tug of me pitched through the restaurant and into the street."

Iris's face lights up. She does not even try to disguise her fascinated delight at this.

I stifle a smile. "Well, would you like a lift back?"

We park half a block from the Caballero, and then walk. There's commotion around the entrance. Several employees are outside picking up some kind of rubble — bits of wood and glass. As we reach the fragments, I realize that they're pieces of the front doors, smithereens all over the sidewalk and street. The doorway is gaping open with just a few splinters of wood remaining at the edges, dangling from bent hinges.

"Was that . . . *you?*" I ask Hercule.

He doesn't reply. He rubs the back of his neck with one hand.

We enter the restaurant to find the whole place recovering from what looks like a tornado. Tables are overturned. Some guests are nursing twisted ankles or bumped heads. I hear several versions of the story breathlessly recounted. Some voices are raw—mostly, I note, from laughter. Several people point to Hercule, and his frown deepens.

My family's table is unscathed but for Hercule's single over-turned chair (which is in one piece, on its side). Apparently he was jerked backwards from it and then catapulted through the restaurant, across the dance floor, and into the hotel lobby, where he obliterated the front doors before launching up the street after me.

As I survey the fracas, my eyes, almost by accident, find the clock above the stage. Fifteen minutes to midnight.

There's Dad, standing next to our table. I rush to him as the Washington Fifteen strikes up a slow waltz in an effort to restore some sense of normality.

"Dad," I say, "could you translate this?" I hold out the photo.

He takes it in hand, and looks. "'I'd forgotten this was written here," he says. He mumbles the words to himself in Spanish, and then says, "To my family. If I could give you life through my death, I would.'"

"What does it mean?" I say.

"It was from a prayer Gonzalo wrote," says my Aunt Ana, approaching us from the other side of the table. "I remember Mother reciting it. He wrote it before he left for the war."

Iris and I share a puzzled glance over what possible connection this prayer could have with Hercule's Noble Weakness. Onstage, Sarena approaches the microphone.

"Thank you, everyone," she says. "Sorry for all the commotion tonight, but we'll keep playing if you keep dancing. This next number is a new one for the band. It's my arrangement. With lyrics by my friend—Gabriela Rivera." She points to me.

Then, the whole population of the restaurant stands. They begin to applaud as the band strikes up the tune, and Sarena sings, her voice clear and strong—my words.

The day you held me close
In springtime showers . . .

As the tune grows, and the dance floor fills, something strange happens. A gentle breeze blows in, through the busted doors. It's fresh and cool, bathing everything.

And it is bursting with the scent of hyacinths, stronger than I've ever smelled it—stronger than I believed possible.

The air crackles with the bite, and drips with the sweetness. My nose itches. My eyes water. Suddenly, I sneeze—and then sneeze again. Around me, I hear other people sneezing, some uncontrollably. To my left, a man doubles over while his wife's eyes swell with allergic tears.

But the smell is too wonderful to resist. I breathe deeply, my whole body suffused with a tingling pleasure, my mind a mess of colliding infatuation even as my sinuses clog. It's more than intoxicating — it's deranging. It's the smell of everything about to begin, the whole of creation on the day of the first sunrise, and I'm filled with an intense, reckless desire — an agony of it. My hands grasp the air, hunting for something. Sylvester's phantom is before me, evoked from memory with a greed for detail I didn't think I possessed. If he were here, I would put my arms around him. Pull him to me. I would bite his lips. I would —

There's a commotion off to the side, and I turn to see through watering eyes something that I did not expect. It's Iris and Wendy, mere feet away. They're locked together in a passionate embrace. Iris has pulled Wendy to her. She's kissing her, both of them sneezing —

Then I see my own parents, at our table, making out like teenagers. Mom is sitting on Dad's lap. Dad's hands are everywhere, pulling Mom's dress from her shoulders. Mom is kissing the nape of his neck, tangling her fingers in his hair —

"Such strange powers — *ah-tchoo!*" Sarena sings, trying to continue as her eyes turn red and sneeze after sneeze possesses her, "in the smell of blooming flowers. Nothing mine — *ah-tchoo!* — and nothing — *ah-tchoo!* — yours — it all was ours . . ."

I turn to Hercule. He's sitting calmly in his special chair amid the uproar, looking about with a mildly amused expression. I take another breath of the narcotic air, and nearly swoon with desire. I can scarcely believe what's happening. It is bedlam! Milo Stathopoulos is holding hands with Jeff Dounais. There's Ms. Lime and . . . Mr. Hale? I turn away, blushing, and see my Mom's parents, the Mason-Hunts . . . they're . . . *goodness!*

"Hergyule!" I shout through my stuffed and running nose, "are you *baygig* dis *habbedh?"* I'm laughing and crying simultaneously as the passionate melee tumbles around us.

"I don't *make* things happen," says Hercule.

"Budh you *are* baygig dis habbedh!" I say, and sneeze twice into my sleeve.

Hercule nods.

I know what the last words of Sarena's song are, since I wrote them. But she doesn't quite get them out of her mouth. Just before she finishes, after an especially epic sneeze, someone leaps onto the stage — it's Raahi. He knocks the microphone off its stand. He grabs Sarena by the shoulders, but before he can kiss her, she kisses him, diving impatiently past his advances. The two of them stumble, then fall headlong from the stage onto the dance floor, oblivious, rolling over the boards.

As the ecstatically debilitated band plays the last few chords of the song (and I see one of the saxophone players inexplicably playing a trombone, and vice versa), Hercule stands slowly. His gray clothes waft up around him. He holds out his long arms, like the giant boughs of a tree, and a new wind washes in, slow and broad. It is crisp, clean, scentless. My racing pulse slows as the perfume clears from the restaurant, and I take a quick survey of the couplings joined in the past minutes. It seems everyone in the place is embracing tenderly, most in pairs but some in groups of three, four, or more. No one appears embarrassed. Even Ms. Lime and Mr. Hale are holding hands, Ms. Lime's two sons looking bemusedly at them.

Hercule raises his arms further, for attention. Everyone quietly gazes at him, awestruck and in love.

He gestures to the clock above the stage. It is midnight.

He motions to me to stand before him, and I approach. Around me, my friends and family converge, pressing gently forward, forming a ring. Hercule's clothes, though torn by his tumble in the street, are arranged correctly now, and his face is serious. "Are you ready, Gabriela?" he asks.

"No," I reply.

He extends his hand.

I reach out. I curl my fingers around his.

A chill races through me.

I take a surprised breath —

silver

I open my eyes without realizing I'd closed them. I see
my parents first, then Iris, Sarena, and Raahi, all staring at me
with a terrible awe on their faces.

I look down at myself, my clothes, my hands. Silver. A lock
of my blanched hair floats up before me, coaxed by an unseen
current. I lift my hand to brush it away and feel the very air
resisting the motion, thick as water.

Hercule regards me coolly as I come to my senses.

"Hello, sir," I croak. "And . . . welcome . . . welcome to
. . ." I'm trying to say what Gonzalo said to him, but I can't.
I'm having trouble pushing the air through my lungs. I'm not
breathing.

No sooner does this occur to me than I notice the strange,
profound stillness of my body. My heart has stopped.

"*Oh,*" I say.

"No hurry now," says Hercule.

"Gabriela?" says Iris. She steps forward. I grasp both her hands, and find them neither warm nor cold. Touching them is like touching a pair of gloves.

Friends and family around us, Hercule and I head out through the shattered front doors of the hotel. Soon we're all standing together on the sidewalk. I turn to Hercule.

"Yes, Gabriela?" he says. "What is it?"

With some difficulty, I push air through my lungs and speak. "Don't forget . . . your chair," I say.

"Oh! Yes, thanks." He disappears inside, emerging a moment later carrying the heavy thing with some difficulty.

"Dad?" I say, turning. Dad steps forward, his eyes scared, tears pouring down. "Would you . . . give us a lift?"

I help Hercule maneuver the chair onto the roof. Dad has some rope in the back, and we pass it through the rolled-down windows and tie it. Then we all cram into the car — Hercule and I again in the backwards seats way back — and begin to drive. Behind us, other cars file in, and a motorcade forms, snaking through town to the narrow road, the pine forest, and the fog. With the night, there's nothing to be seen beyond manifold red embers of taillights and the white beacons of headlights.

The procession enters the pitch-black parking lot. Most people leave their engines running and lights on, striping the public Fields with yellow. We untie Hercule's chair and walk slowly, finding our steps. Hercule leads the way. He struggles with the chair, which seems at every turn to confound his attempts to carry it, but he is remarkably sure-footed in the darkness.

"Can you see in the dark?" Iris asks him abruptly.

"I have a sense similar to that possessed by sharks," he replies. He gestures to the twin gill slits on either side of his nose.

"Sharks?" says Iris.

"We're related to hammerheads."

"How can you be related to *sharks?*" says Iris. "Deaths are supernatural."

"*Mostly* supernatural," says Hercule. "The rest is shark."

There are lots of people here to see me off; some of them had the foresight to bring flashlights, or lighters, or candles, which lend a spectral glow to the dark Fields, especially as we proceed to the rockier, more uneven ground farther from the parking lot. Sarena and Wendy approach a group of kids all dressed in their marching band uniforms. Someone hands Sarena her trumpet, and Wendy her flute, and the band strikes up, playing a slow version of one of the tunes they perform at football games. Sad "Tequila." The crowd gathers behind Hercule and me, following us onto the grass. Sarena leads her band alongside, instruments glittering.

As we cross the rougher field, each member of my immediate family stoops to pick up a stone. As a kid I wondered — if every family member who passes takes one stone to stack next to the boundary, and this has gone on basically forever, won't the field eventually run out? Yet there seems no shortage.

Finally, we reach the sign: DEPARTURE.

The turf to the edge is mowed and trampled. Beyond lies shadowy, waist-high grass. Ranged all along the edge are the cairns, in broad, sloping piles and neat stacks. Some appear recent. Others are half-swallowed by dirt and age.

Hercule and I face into the darkness, brushing the long grass with our fingers. The high field continues uphill out of sight. I find myself thinking back on my visit here with Sylvester—both of us kept out by the forces that now stand ready to admit me.

Hercule puts his chair down with a relieved sigh. He and I turn and face the crowd.

departure

My family stands off to one side — Mom and Dad;
Aunt Ana, Hector, and their kids; and Mom's parents — but
everyone else lines up before me. There's a standard script and
procedure here. It isn't required, but everyone knows it, and it
makes things easier. Ms. Lime is first, wearing an expression
that suggests she didn't plan this.

"Thank you for being my friend, Ms. Lime," I recite.

"Thank you for being mine, Gabriela," she says. We hug,
and she steps aside for the next person: Mr. Hale. He hands me
a bouquet of lotus flowers. As soon as he releases them into
my hands, they turn from red blooms on green stems to silver
blooms on gray stems.

"Thank you for being my friend, Mr. Hale," I say.

"Thank you for being mine, Gabriela," he says hoarsely.

"And thank you for being Raahi's," I say.

"Who?"

"You met him, at the wake. He's here now. He decided not to comply with the draft."

This strikes Mr. Hale deeply. "Thank you for telling me that," he says. Then, "Gabriela, if you *do* see Sylvester . . ."

"I'll remind him," I say.

Mr. Hale steps aside, and I hand the blooms to Hercule.

Father Ernesto is next. He's holding a glass chalice of blessed oil, which glows like liquid gold in the flashlight beams. He's here to administer Extreme Unction, a practice somewhat debated within the Church: considering that I'm technically dead now, theologians disagree about whether the destination of my soul can be affected by the sacraments. But the Pope said that those churches employing Extreme Unction during departures can continue — there's no harm.

"If you'd like, Gabriela," he says.

I know that Dad, watching off to the side, will be comforted, and I bow my head. Father Ernesto dips his fingers in the oil and recites, "Through this holy unction and His own most tender mercy, may the Lord pardon you whatever sins you have committed, by sight — " I close my eyes, and Father Ernesto smears oil on my lids — "by hearing" — he daubs oil on my ears — "by smell" — he anoints the tip of my nose — "by taste" — he touches my lips — "by touch" — I hold out my hands, and he puts oil in each palm — "or by walking." He kneels slowly on his bad old knees and puts a drop of oil on each of my gray shoes. He makes the sign of the cross in the air before me and delivers the benediction: "The Lord bless you and keep you, Gabriela. The Lord make His face shine upon you, and be gracious unto you. The Lord lift up His countenance upon you and give you peace."

"Thank you for being my friend, Jaime," I say.

"Thank you for being mine, Gabriela," he says. "And— thank you for the times we have disagreed."

"There will be more," I say.

Other faces proceed past—the very large Milo Stathopoulos, his eyes moist (he's as surprised as I am that he's upset) and several other acquaintances from school. Iris's parents arrive together, and Raahi's mom.

Next are Sarena and Raahi, together. They're holding hands, and they look at me solemnly.

"Thank you for being my friend, Sarena. Thank you, Raahi," I say.

"Thank you for being mine, Gabriela!" Sarena squeaks. We hug, and she shivers—I think I'm cold to the touch.

"Thank you for being mine, Gabriela," says Raahi. I hug him. He says, "I know you'll come back. You won't comply." He smiles.

There is one more person at the end of the line: Iris. She approaches me, tears shining in her eyes. She's holding something in one hand—fabric. She holds it up so I can see. It's a white dress. "For when you return," she says. She still believes it could happen. I think of Gonzalo's prayer—"If I could give you life through my death, I would." It's not too late. I can still figure it out.

I open my mouth to speak, but my throat is suddenly narrow. Iris can't speak either. I brush the tears from her cheeks with my cold fingers.

"I'll wait for you here," she says finally. She steps to the side to stand with the rest of the public, a few paces distant.

Now, it's my family's turn.

Dad's brown suit is rumpled, and Mom's cardigan doesn't seem nearly warm enough. They each hold a flashlight in one hand and a small stone in the other. Their eyes are bright with tears. Aunt Ana and Hector stand beside them, Ana holding Pia in her arms, Hector holding Juan's hand.

And my grandparents, the Mason-Hunts. They approach first, knowing, I suppose, that their goodbyes are a little less important to me than the rest. They're stooped and skinny. Their hair is white, their skin pale. They look almost like miniature Deaths themselves.

"Hello, Gabriela," says the old man. The woman nods to me. I take a breath and deliver the script that has, fortunately, been supplied, because I have no idea what else to say to these people, strangers to me for my whole life.

"Leave what you have come to leave," I recite.

"I leave a piece of my heart," says my grandfather, and he kneels with some difficulty and places a stone at my feet.

"A piece of my heart," says my grandmother, and she places her stone.

"A piece of my heart goes with you also," I say. But it doesn't — I'm honestly confused about their presence here, about why they would want to attend my death, having missed my life. "Did my mom ask you to come?" I say, as they begin to turn away.

"We wanted to meet you," says my grandfather.

"You've had plenty of opportunities before this," I say. "I thought you hated me."

"We don't hate you, Gabriela," says my grandmother.

"Well, after I get my Pardon, you should come over for dinner," I say.

My grandfather nods. I sound almost like when I chastised my parents. Why am I the one to teach all of these adults how to behave? These two, who resemble a sagging version of the imperious couple in the photo on my desk. They are tired, old, regretful. They step aside. "I'll see you later," I say.

My aunt and uncle and their kids approach next.

"Leave what you have come to leave," I recite.

"I leave a piece of my heart," says my aunt, and she kneels and places a stone at my feet. Pia drops the little pebble she's been given. Hector and Juan follow.

"A piece of my heart goes with you also," I say to them.

Finally, my parents. The three of us hug for a long time. Mom's arms nearly crush me. When we separate, she looks at me tenderly. "You're the best daughter I could imagine," she says. She kneels and places her stone. "I leave my heart here," she says, her voice suddenly slipping. Dad places his next to hers, leaned against it. His breath rattles. "Come back," he stutters. "That's . . . that's *final*."

They step away.

Hercule and I turn from the gathered, silent crowd. Sarena strikes up the band again, and they play, roughly, the song she sang at the Caballero. She begins the tune, and her voice is steady, ringing across the Fields.

Hercule lifts his chair, and we step across the boundary. I leave my life.

the oaks

I'm not sure how much time passes after that. One step follows another through the blackness, Hercule grunting under the weight of his chair.

Eventually, the brushing blades of the long grass diminish, and I find myself staring down at low turf, clarifying in a new, thin light. It seems like morning is coming, but that much time can't have passed already, can it? Small yellow flowers peek from scrubby green grass. Then—blue, purple, and white flowers emerge in clusters from thick stalks. I look around, wondering. The flowers are everywhere, continuing up the rise in dense multicolor groups. I take a deep breath, but I can't smell anything.

"Are these hyacinths?" I ask.

"Yes," says Hercule, laboring under his chair. "Quite abundant here." He places the chair roughly on the ground and leans against it.

"Why don't you let me carry that for a while?" I say.

"I thought you would never ask," he replies.

"Is it old?" I lay my hands on the low back.

"No. I've had it about five years."

"You sure were upset about losing it."

"It is my favorite chair."

I lift it and carry it sideways, by its back and one leg, and we start up the hill again. The hyacinths continue for a while but diminish in number as we near the top of the rise.

The light increases. The blue sky is textured with a fine tulle of stretched clouds. Soon, we crest the hill and stand at the start of a short plain, which leads to a sparse but healthy grove of old oaks straight ahead, a few green buds beginning at the tips of recently dormant branchlets, casting a net of shadow on a floor of rusting leaves. To the left a rough, rocky outcropping mounds up. Swallows fly here, swooping, looking for bugs or playing.

"The Oaks," I whisper. I've heard about them my whole life, and now here they are. The very end of everything. I'm about to say something more when I'm distracted by a startling revelation.

"My *clothes!*" I exclaim. I am totally naked.

"Yes, it happened at the top of the rise," says Hercule.

"But you still have yours," I say. It seems a little unfair.

"I am not dead."

Now that his chair is jouncing against my bare skin, it's even more uncomfortable to carry.

"Um, could we *share* this?" I say.

Hercule takes the legs, and I take the back, and we continue.

As we near the Oaks and the rock outcropping, I see we aren't alone. There are two figures ahead, at the edge of the trees. One is extremely tall, a Death. The other I don't recognize at first. He's an old man, fat and naked, the early light gleaming off his hairy shoulders, chest, and bald head. His pendulous stomach lolls, weightless before him. He waves to us when he sees us.

"The Singing Man!" I say. I wave back. "That's Gretchen next to him, isn't it?"

"Yes," says Hercule. Gretchen stands silently, tall as a willow and wearing a form-fitting gray-black dress. Her mass of dark gray hair swims smokelike around her head and shoulders.

"You don't sound pleased to see her," I observe.

"She's been giving me the silent treatment," says Hercule.

"You two know each other?"

"She is my wife."

I blink. *"Married?"* I say. "Has she been worried about you? Since we kidnapped you?"

"I expect it has been a nice vacation for her," says Hercule. He frowns. "I'm not the easiest person to get along with, some say."

"Hello!" the Singing Man calls as we arrive.

"I know you," I tell him. "I saw you outside our school. We called you the Singing Man."

"That's good!" he says pleasantly, with a slight accent. "My name is Alfeo. I see you've come prepared to sit awhile?"

"I'm Gabriela," I say. "This is Hercule."

"Nice to meet you," says Alfeo.

"My friends and I enjoyed your music," I say.

"That was my wrap-up," says Alfeo. "I loved to sing, but I was a salesman for all my life. I wanted finally to realize that dream, just a little. This is Gretchen, my Death," he says.

"Hello, Gretchen," I say. She doesn't reply.

"She won't speak to you," says Hercule icily, "because you're with me." He glares at her, and she glares back.

Hercule and I put the chair down between us.

"What are you still doing here?" I ask Alfeo. "You departed days and days ago."

"Yes, well, she gave me a week to guess her Noble Weakness. But no. Since then, I've been deciding — getting ready." He nods significantly toward the Oaks. "I've walked all around here," he says. "You know what? We don't have to sleep anymore, isn't that nice? Plenty of time, and I stop and talk to everyone."

"But you haven't crossed over," I say.

Alfeo clasps his hands before him, encircling his belly. "It's hard. Singing is one thing — *fah*, I could leave that. But my most sacred — my wife and daughter. I couldn't! Only after talking to other people who came by, I understood I don't have it so hard. I was sixty-seven, you know. Not too bad." He looks at me sadly; I'm an example, I guess, of someone who does have it kind of hard — someone who had less time.

"I saw you on your departure day," I say. "You sang a last song."

"Yes, a great song!" says Alfeo. "A triumphant song!" And he sings it, just as he did then.

> *Vittoria, vittoria, mio core!*
> *Non lagrimar più,*
> *È sciolta d'Amore*
> *La vil servitù.*
> *Nel duol, ne' tormenti*
> *Io più non mi sfaccio*
> *È rotto ogni laccio,*
> *Sparito il timore!*

"You speak Italian?" he asks.

"No, sorry," I say.

"Well, that song says, 'Victorious, my heart! Weep no more! You're no longer Love's servant. Grief and torment don't worry me. Every snare has broken. Fear has disappeared!'" He nods as he goes through the lines in English, approving of them. "I'm glad to have met you, Gabriela," he says. "Now . . ." He turns to Gretchen. "Thank you for your patience."

"I needed none," she replies. Her voice is low, a breathy wisp.

Without hesitation, Alfeo steps into the shadows of the Oaks, walking almost merrily. The air changes around him as he goes, silver, like mercury. He pushes forward, using his arms, wading into the waves of it, and he begins to fade. The ripples increase, roiling around him thick as ropes.

And he's gone. A shimmer remains, then nothing. The swallows chirp in the trees, flutter down to the leaves he just stepped on, and race away on the wing, as if he never passed.

Gretchen, likewise, is gone — disappeared.

"Finally," Hercule mutters.

"Where did Alfeo go?" I ask. "The afterlife?" I stare under the trees. "He couldn't guess her weakness," I say.

"Hers is impossible," says Hercule.

"You know it?"

"Of course." Hercule pauses, then says, "What did you think of that song? It seemed like a good choice, to declare victory."

"Maybe for him," I say. "How can I be victorious? I haven't even fought yet." I pause. "Hey, your *chair!*" I exclaim. It has disappeared from between us without a trace.

Hercule looks a little surprised. "Gretchen took it," he says. "That was nice of her."

I find myself upset that it's gone. My arms are still aching from having carried it all this way. And to have it just vanish . . .

Suddenly, I'm crying. It's funny, I haven't shed a single tear this whole time, but losing Hercule's chair has somehow set me off. He stands quietly next to me, saying nothing, while I weep. I put my face in my hands. Each breath, which I don't need anymore to live, is used for more tears. Then Hercule says, "Someone's coming."

I lift my head, wiping my cheeks.

There's a sound from our left, by the rock outcropping.

"This place is busy," says Hercule. "You'd think there was a war on."

"Sylvester!" I shout.

He's already seen me. When he arrives, we're both awkward, looking at each other's naked, silver bodies.

"You're beautiful," I say, speaking the words as I think them, which leaves me a bit embarrassed.

"You, too," he says.

"I saw your father," I say. "He told me to tell you he loves you." Sylvester is so gorgeous, it's not easy to let my eyes rest on him.

"I waited for you again," says Sylvester.

I'm a little startled as I recognize Hercule's Hint from Sylvester's list — "Wait for Gabriela." I still don't know why.

I look under the Oaks, at the dappled shadows there, which are growing more firm as the light around us grows stronger. Sunrise will come soon. I find myself thinking about Gonzalo's prayer. "If I could give you life through my death . . ."

And perhaps something starts to come together.

"Hercule," I say, "you told me my grandfather gave his Pardon to someone he was with."

"Did I?" says Hercule.

"Yes, you . . . Well, no. You never did quite say that." I turn to Sylvester. "Sylvester, I think I have something for you. I didn't know it until just now. It's unclaimed, isn't it, Hercule? *That's* why there was a blank next to it, in the archives. Gonzalo gave his Pardon to his family — to me. To give life through his death."

"That's correct, Gabriela," says Hercule. "But consider carefully. 'To my family,' he said. His intent was that it be passed to his descendants. It is *yours* to use."

I ponder this. "Hercule," I say, "what did you think of my grandparents, when you saw them today?"

"Eh? Who?" Hercule frowns.

"My mom's parents, the Mason-Hunts — they attended my departure."

"I suppose I thought nothing of them," he says.

"Did you know I'd never met them before?" I ask. "They disowned Mom when she and Dad married."

"For what reason?" Hercule asks.

"Because Dad is Mexican," I say. "And mom's parents, the Mason-Hunts, they're part of me — *that* kind of family is half of me. Family as a kind of . . . a kind of uniform. Family that divides everything into Us and Them. Maybe it's about skin color, or religion, or who you fall in love with . . . it's all Us and Them. But I can't accept that. Not after everything that's happened to me, to my parents—my friends. And I know that Gonzalo's gift had nothing to do with that. That's not who he was, and it's not who I am. He would have wanted me to reach out. To help someone in need, whoever they are."

"'Each of you should use whatever gift you have received to serve others,'" says Hercule.

"That's right!" I say, surprised to hear St. Mary's motto—the very verse that inspired my Wrap-Up List in the first place. "And you knew all along that I'd do it," I say, "even though you're pretending otherwise. Did I tell you that I saw Sylvester's Wrap-Up List? He'd asked you about signing up for the army, and your Hint said, 'Volunteer.'"

"That is the usual way of going about it."

"But he wasn't eighteen yet. He departed before his birthday, so the Hint didn't make sense. But now it does; he's old enough now." I pause. "This has been it all along. I have one last gift to give away."

Sylvester is watching the back-and-forth between us like a mouse watching an argument between cats.

"Are you sure then?" says Hercule.

"I'm sure," I say.

Hercule turns abruptly to Sylvester. "Young man," he says, "you are hereby granted the Pardon first earned by Gabriela's grandfather. It has been transferred to you. Return to your life, and live well."

Sylvester looks confused. "You're . . . letting me go?" he says.

Hercule continues: "Your father is out of town right now, visiting his sister. But he left the side door unlocked." He observes Sylvester strictly, trying to discern if anything is sinking in. "You listening?" he asks. "I will also point out, though Gabriela has already done so, that you are eighteen now."

"Eighteen," Sylvester echoes.

Hercule shakes his head. "A few steps down the hill may revive you," he says, gesturing back the way we came. Sylvester looks at me. He looks at his bare feet.

Then, he takes a step downhill.

He gasps.

Air fills his lungs, and his body wrests itself away from death. Color floods into his chest and down through his arms and legs. His hair falls, plastering his skull as if he's just been pulled from a dunk tank. He shudders, and then sobs. *"Gabriela . . ."* he croaks.

"Iris is waiting at the Departure point," I say. "She brought some extra clothes." I turn away from him. It's too hard to look. I lock my gaze under the Oaks.

"Thank you," he says, the words drenched in insufficiency.

He takes another step downhill, and then another. I listen as he retreats, straining my ears until there's nothing left.

the last dance

"That was foolish," says Hercule.

"But you knew I would do it," I say. "You told Sylvester to wait for me. You told him to volunteer."

Hercules shakes his head. "I can only encourage things——"

"That *might* happen, I know," I say.

"You're like your grandfather, Gabriela, in that way——generous to a fault," says Hercule.

"I'm glad to be like him," I say. "But I'm not dying under an olive tree."

"That's why I called you foolish." Hercule seems a little mystified by it all——he's calling me a fool, but he says it gently. "Anyway, it makes no difference to me. I already suffered my Abeyance."

"Is that when Deaths disappear after they grant Pardons?"

"Indeed."

"What is it?" I ask. "Is it bad?"

"Yes," says Hercule, "but you wouldn't understand."

"Well, is it a tragedy or just an inconvenience?" I ask.

"It is between the two," says Hercule. "In the case of your grandfather, I didn't suffer too badly." He looks at me soberly. "You know, Gabriela, much of what has happened here has been important for me. It's been a long time since I've enjoyed an opportunity to see through such a splendid wrap-up. Kisses — and each one important in a different way. It was quite ingenious."

"You're welcome," I reply. And I am glad, I really am. But it's not enough. "Hercule, why did you pick me?" I ask. "In school we always learn that it's random. But this wasn't random — it can't be."

"Anything can be random," said Hercule. "That's the nature of randomness." He pauses. "But no, it wasn't quite. A few days after I'd been attached to your friend Sylvester, your name came up — Felix was going to get it. I called in a favor he owed me, and he handed you over. It was nagging at me, I suppose, to have this unused Pardon floating around."

The triviality of this tale strikes me kind of hard. My whole story is reduced to Hercule feeling "nagged." I wish it could have been something more important. I look away down the hill. "What if I just ran off? Ran back home?" I say.

"You'll find you can't take even a single step," says Hercule. "The forces that prevent others from coming here will prevent you from leaving. But you can console yourself that you accomplished much of what you set out to do. A victory that might be quite freeing, as your friend Alfeo suggested."

"I'm barely sixteen."

"I know," says Hercule. "I'm sorry, Gabriela. I agree, you are young."

I look under the Oaks and imagine my grandfather, all those years before I was born, staring into the Tunisian olive grove.

"Hercule," I say, "you told me to save you a dance. But I don't really know how to dance." I step up to him, hugely tall before me.

He takes my small gray hands in his enormous silver ones. "A waltz," he says, and begins, setting the tempo with a tuneless little *tum-tee-tee, tum-tee-tee*. The two of us turn in a slow circle, at the very edge of everything. The predawn glow has increased around us, evaporating the mist hanging above the turf, turning the grass brilliant green. The tanned oak leaves shine with dew. The swallows flit across the field.

"Goodbye, Hercule," I say. "Thank you for being my friend."

"Thank you, Gabriela. I was proud to escort you."

I release his hands.

I look under the Oaks, observing as the shadows continue to sharpen with the approach of dawn.

Then I turn away from them. Downhill—toward home.

Hercule blanches, and an annoyed expression crosses his face. *"Gabriela,"* he says strictly, "don't embarrass yourself."

"You're right that my grandfather was noble and generous," I say. "But I think he was also kind of tricky."

I close my eyes.

I lift one bare foot, and take a step downhill.

No force prevents me.

As my heel sinks into the grass, a sudden clap of thunder cracks in my chest, and I gasp, inhaling. I look down to see my gray skin flood with color, starting at my belly and spilling through my arms and legs. Another crash reverberates. It's my heart beating.

My hair falls straight down, slapping my shoulders, soaking wet. The thick air around me evaporates, and I stumble.

"Stop!" Hercule yells. He holds out his long arms commandingly.

I turn to him, shivering and thrilled, breathless. *"I figured it out!"* I shout, laughing. "Your Noble Weakness is *giving away a Pardon!* That's what Iris found — everyone who ever earned a Pardon from you transferred it. They promised it to someone else, didn't they? Just like Gonzalo did — promising his to his descendants."

"But — but — " Hercule stutters.

"Only this time was different. This time — it was more complicated. The Pardon I gave away and the Pardon I earned weren't the same. I gave away Gonzalo's Pardon, to

Sylvester — and because of your Noble Weakness, that generous act earned me a new one. Which I'm using for *myself*."

Hercule's eyes are wide in startled shock as I explain.

Suddenly the sun breaks over the horizon, throwing my sharp, solid shadow far ahead of me down the slope. "I really meant it, by the way, Hercule — about you being a good friend. And I'm truly sorry to do this to you."

He stares at me silently, rage and confusion smoldering in his eyes.

"I hope this is an inconvenience, and not a tragedy. Um — will you be able to sit in your favorite chair during your Abeyance?" I know I'm needling him a little. I can't help it.

For a moment, it looks like he won't respond. Finally, he nods. "Yes," he says icily, "I will be able to sit in my favorite chair." And then he vanishes, blinking out as quickly as a slammed door, and I'm alone.

I glance under the Oaks, where the firm, dark shadows lie upon the rust leaves. My eyes linger for a moment, but there's nothing for me there. Not yet, anyway.

I turn downhill.

After two or three steps walking, I break into a run. The grass is wet, freezing on my bare feet, but it doesn't slow me. I'm rushing, my breath deep and strong. Up ahead, two figures come into view down by the departure point. I yell to them, and they see me and wave. Iris is there, with Sylvester next to her, wearing the white dress she brought for me. It fits him badly.

I pass the hyacinths, and their scent fills my lungs, tickling my nose. It's not the impossible soup that Hercule brought to the Caballero—it's just flowers, fresh, sweet, stinging, and alive.

I suddenly remember Hercule's Hint to me.

—*The Fields.*

I am ready to be kissed.

live for today.

TRANSCRIPTION FROM OFFICIAL
DOCUMENTS
PROVIDED BY: ELLIS COUNTY DEPARTURE
AUTHORITY
Attending Death: Hercule
Site: Ellis Fields, Oak Grove
Departing Person: Gabriela Rivera. Citizenship: USA
Departure Status: *Pardon 1. Trns. from Gonzalo
Rivera; Re-Trns. to Sylvester Hale
Pardon 2. Granted and used

*See attached article for further information. Iris Van
Voorhees, "The Departure of Gabriela Rivera," *Journal of
the Association of Departure Science*, vol. 96, no. 7.

acknowledgments

The humble first draft I produced of this story had the wonderful fortune to benefit from the help of several first-rate minds. I'm particularly grateful to my agent, Jenni Ferrari-Adler, who had the patience to steer me through draft after draft of my strange affinity for wrong directions. I'd also like to thank Margaret Raymo at Houghton Mifflin for her solid advice throughout the editing process — it was wonderful to have such wise guidance at the moment the book gained its final shape. But most of all I'm indebted to my wife, Anne, for talking everything through with me again and again. Anne, you continue to be the greatest influence on the way I live and think. I count myself very lucky to have such help as I muddle through this life.